P9-DHG-287
THIS... IS REAL PAIN!
THE ADVENTURES OF
SPIDER-MAN
SINISTER INTENTIONS

THE ADVENTURES OF SPIDER-MAN
SINISTER INTENTIONS

NEL YOMTOV, RALPH MACCHIO & MICHAEL HIGGINS
WRITERS

ALEX SAVIUK, BEN HERRERA & ANDY KUHN
PENCILERS

ROBERT STULL, MIKE S. MILLER & DON HUDSON
INKERS

KEVIN TINSLEY, MATT WEBB & MALIBU
COLORISTS

STEVE DUTRO & MICHAEL HIGGINS
LETTERERS

JOE ANDREANI
ASSISTANT EDITOR

SARRA MOSSOFF & MARK POWERS
EDITORS

JOHN ROMITA SR.
FRONT COVER ARTIST

SPIDER-MAN CREATED BY **STAN LEE & STEVE DITKO**

COLLECTION EDITOR **MARK D. BEAZLEY**
ASSISTANT EDITOR **CAITLIN O'CONNELL**
ASSOCIATE MANAGING EDITOR **KATERI WOODY**
ASSOCIATE MANAGER, DIGITAL ASSETS **JOE HOCHSTEIN**
SENIOR EDITOR, SPECIAL PROJECTS **JENNIFER GRÜNWALD**
VP PRODUCTION & SPECIAL PROJECTS **JEFF YOUNGQUIST**
RESEARCH **GARY HENDERSON**
LAYOUT **JEPH YORK**
PRODUCTION **COLORTEK**

BOOK DESIGNER **ADAM DEL RE**

SVP PRINT, SALES & MARKETING **DAVID GABRIEL**
DIRECTOR, LICENSED PUBLISHING **SVEN LARSEN**

EDITOR IN CHIEF **C.B. CEBULSKI**
CHIEF CREATIVE OFFICER **JOE QUESADA**
PRESIDENT **DAN BUCKLEY**
EXECUTIVE PRODUCER **ALAN FINE**

ADVENTURES OF SPIDER-MAN: SINISTER INTENTIONS. Contains material originally published in magazine form as ADVENTURES OF SPIDER-MAN #1-6 and ADVENTURES OF THE X-MEN #3. First printing 2019. ISBN 978-1-302-91779-1. Published by MARVEL WORLDWIDE, INC., a subsidiary of MARVEL ENTERTAINMENT, LLC. OFFICE OF PUBLICATION: 135 West 50th Street, New York, NY 10020. **Printed in Canada.** DAN BUCKLEY, President, Marvel Entertainment; JOHN NEE, Publisher; JOE QUESADA, Chief Creative Officer; TOM BREVOORT, SVP of Publishing; DAVID BOGART, Associate Publisher & SVP of Talent Affairs; DAVID GABRIEL, SVP of Sales & Marketing, Publishing; JEFF YOUNGQUIST, VP of Production & Special Projects; DAN CARR, Executive Director of Publishing Technology; ALEX MORALES, Director of Publishing Operations; DAN EDINGTON, Managing Editor; SUSAN CRESPI, Production Manager; STAN LEE, Chairman Emeritus. For information regarding advertising in Marvel Comics or on Marvel.com, please contact Vit DeBellis, Custom Solutions & Integrated Advertising Manager, at vdebellis@marvel.com. For Marvel subscription inquiries, please call 888-511-5480. **Manufactured between 4/12/2019 and 5/14/2019 by SOLISCO PRINTERS, SCOTT, QC, CANADA.**

10 9 8 7 6 5 4 3 2 1

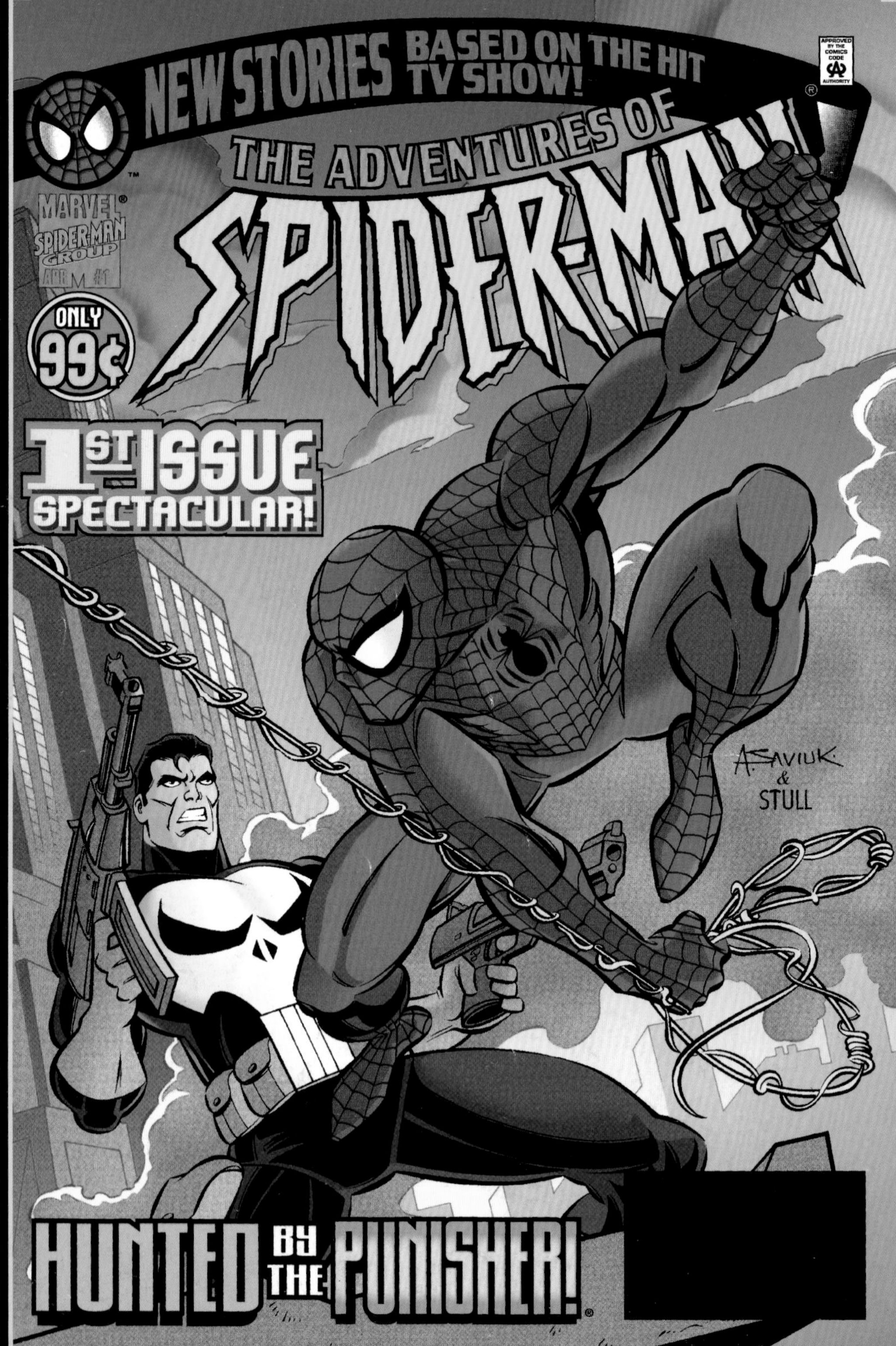
NEW STORIES BASED ON THE HIT TV SHOW!
APPROVED BY THE COMICS CODE AUTHORITY
THE ADVENTURES OF
SPIDER-MAN
MARVEL
SPIDER-MAN GROUP
APR
#1
ONLY 99¢
1ST ISSUE SPECTACULAR!
A. SAVIUK & STULL
HUNTED BY THE PUNISHER!

BITTEN BY A RADIOACTIVE SPIDER, COLLEGE STUDENT PETER PARKER GAINED THE PROPORTIONATE STRENGTH AND AGILITY OF A SPIDER! ARMED WITH HIS WONDROUS WEB-SHOOTERS AND COMMITTED TO USING HIS AMAZING POWERS FOR GOOD, HE STRUGGLES WITH SINISTER SUPER-VILLAINS, MAKING ENDS MEET, AND MAINTAINING SOME SEMBLANCE OF A NORMAL LIFE!
HERE NOW, BASED ON HIS ANIMATED TELEVISION SERIES, ARE... THE ADVENTURES OF SPIDER-MAN
WHEN THE WIND CHILL FACTOR KICKS INTO AN ALREADY BITTER COLD FEBRUARY AFTERNOON, EVEN THE STAUNCHEST CITY DWELLER FEELS IT...
...ESPECIALLY WHEN HE'S SOARING A COUPLE OF HUNDRED FEET ABOVE GROUND LEVEL!
BRRR! I'M FREEZIN'! THESE NEW YORK WINTERS ARE :sniff: KILLERS!
FIRST CHANCE I GET, I'VE GOTTA :sniff: SEW A PAIR OF THERMAL UNDIES INTO MY :sniff: COSTUME!
WEATHER SURE ISN'T DOING ANYTHING FOR THIS :sniff: WICKED HEAD COLD I HAVE, EITHER...
WHAT'S THE USE OF COMPLAINING? AFTER ALL, THIS IS THE PLACE I LOVE-- THE PLACE I CALL HOME...
SHOT IN THE DARK
NEL YOMTOV WRITER
ALEX SAVIUK PENCILER
ROB STULL INKER
STEVE DUTRO LETTERER
KEVIN TINSLEY COLORS
SARRA MOSSOFF EDITOR
BOB BUDIANSKY EDITOR IN CHIEF

:sniff: STILL, IT'S COLD, GREY DAYS LIKE THIS THAT MAKE NEW YORK FEEL SO :sniff: INDIFFERENT... SO CALLOUS AND UNCARING.
JUST ASK THOSE GUYS...
HOME-LESS. DOWN ON THEIR LUCK. THEY REALLY HAVE IT TOUGH.
HNNF! WITH ALL THE CRIME-BUSTIN' WE SUPER HEROES GET THE HEADLINES FOR, THERE ARE STILL BIG PROBLEMS :sniff: THAT WE JUST CAN'T SEEM TO SOLVE...
WELL, MAYBE I CAN DO A LITTLE SOMETHING...
HEADS UP, FELLAS! DON'T LET THE STICKY STUFF HIT YA!
LOOKIT! THAT'S SPIDER-MAN!
HE'S MAKIN' US A HOUSE OUTTA HIS WEBBIN'!
THAT OUGHTA KEEP US A LITTLE WARMER!
SURE WILL, FELLA, BUT I'VE GOTTA KEEP MOVIN' IN THIS COLD. THINK I'LL SEE WHAT'S SHAKIN' OVER BY THE WEST SIDE DOCKS.
TAKE CARE, GUYS! HANG IN!

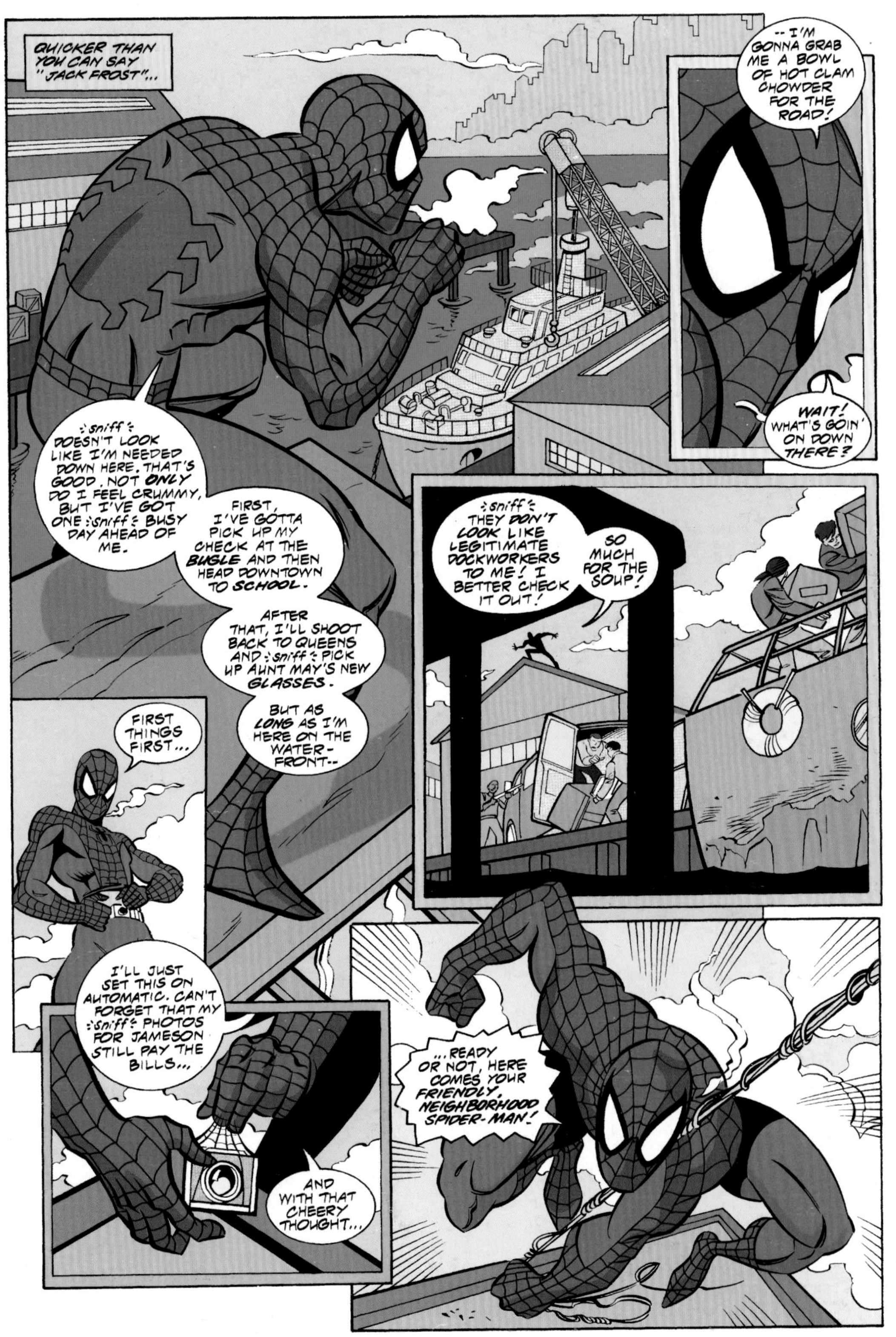
QUICKER THAN YOU CAN SAY "JACK FROST"...
--I'M GONNA GRAB ME A BOWL OF HOT CLAM CHOWDER FOR THE ROAD!
WAIT! WHAT'S GOIN' ON DOWN THERE?
sniff DOESN'T LOOK LIKE I'M NEEDED DOWN HERE. THAT'S GOOD. NOT ONLY DO I FEEL CRUMMY, BUT I'VE GOT ONE sniff BUSY DAY AHEAD OF ME.
FIRST, I'VE GOTTA PICK UP MY CHECK AT THE BUGLE AND THEN HEAD DOWNTOWN TO SCHOOL.
AFTER THAT, I'LL SHOOT BACK TO QUEENS AND sniff PICK UP AUNT MAY'S NEW GLASSES.
BUT AS LONG AS I'M HERE ON THE WATER-FRONT--
sniff THEY DON'T LOOK LIKE LEGITIMATE DOCKWORKERS TO ME! I BETTER CHECK IT OUT!
SO MUCH FOR THE SOUP!
FIRST THINGS FIRST...
I'LL JUST SET THIS ON AUTOMATIC. CAN'T FORGET THAT MY sniff PHOTOS FOR JAMESON STILL PAY THE BILLS...
AND WITH THAT CHEERY THOUGHT...
...READY OR NOT, HERE COMES YOUR FRIENDLY, NEIGHBORHOOD SPIDER-MAN!

DIDN'T YOUR MOTHER EVER TELL YOU TO STAY AWAY FROM THE DOCKS, JUNIOR?
SPROING
THUD
I KNOW I NAILED HIM GOOD, BUT THIS HEAD COLD'S MESSED UP MY TIMING!
IF I WAS AT 100%, I WOULD'VE TAKEN OUT THE CLOWN BEHIND ME IN THE SAME MOVE!
DANNY--!
EAGGHH!
THRACK
WATCH HOW YOU TALK 'BOUT OUR MUTHAS, PUNK! THEY'RE REGULAR SAINTS, Y'KNOW!
UNNGH!
LET ME MESS WID HIM NOW!
WHAMP
WEAKER THAN I THOUGHT! CAN'T LET THEM--
--ARCK!

LET'S FINISH 'IM!
I SAY NO! WE DIDN'T HAVE ORDERS TO WASTE ANYBODY!
YEAH, C'MON! WHAT ABOUT YOU, TELLY?
WE LOADED THE TRUCK LIKE WE WERE SUPPOSED TO-- NOW LET'S BEAT IT!
UNNNHH
CAN'T LET THEM SLIP AWAY...
GOTTA TRY ANY-THING...
H-HEY!
WHOA!
THWIP
THWIP
THAT DOES IT! BLOW 'IM AWAY!
DIE, YOU LITTLE--
NOO!
OH, GOD--!
DON'T DRAG HIM INTO THIS, SCUM--
W-WHO--?!

ENOUGH OF YOUR BLOODSUCKING-- IT'S PAYBACK TIME!
--LET'S SETTLE THIS BETWEEN YOU AND ME!
LOOK AT HIS HARDWARE! HE'LL BLOW US TO SHREDS!
WE GOTTA GET OUTTA HERE! SPLIT UP!

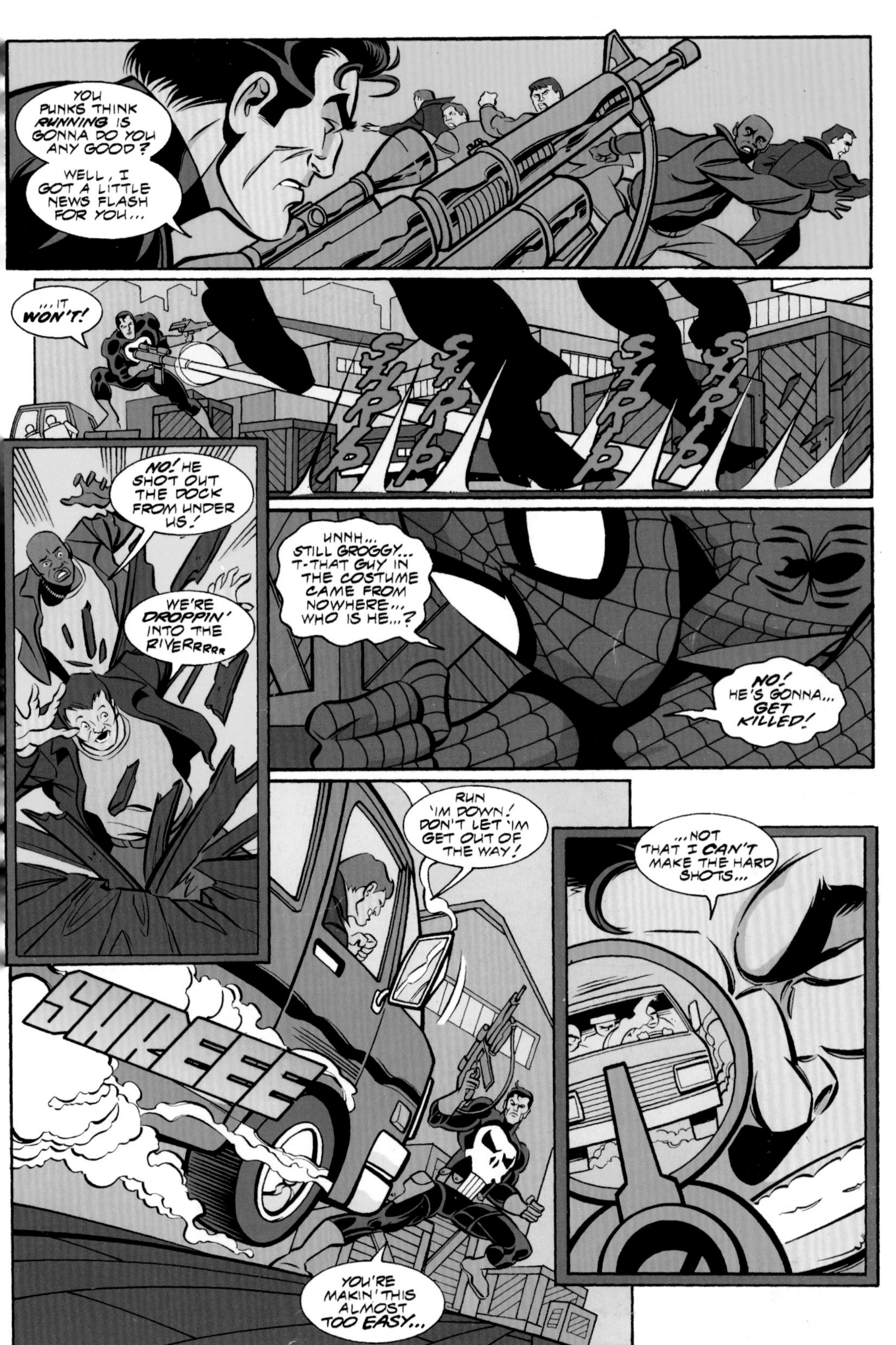
YOU PUNKS THINK RUNNING IS GONNA DO YOU ANY GOOD?
WELL, I GOT A LITTLE NEWS FLASH FOR YOU...
...IT WON'T!
NO! HE SHOT OUT THE DOCK FROM UNDER US!
WE'RE DROPPIN' INTO THE RIVERrrrr
UNNH... STILL GROGGY... T-THAT GUY IN THE COSTUME CAME FROM NOWHERE... WHO IS HE...?
NO! HE'S GONNA... GET KILLED!
SHREEE
RUN 'IM DOWN! DON'T LET 'IM GET OUT OF THE WAY!
YOU'RE MAKIN' THIS ALMOST TOO EASY...
...NOT THAT I CAN'T MAKE THE HARD SHOTS...

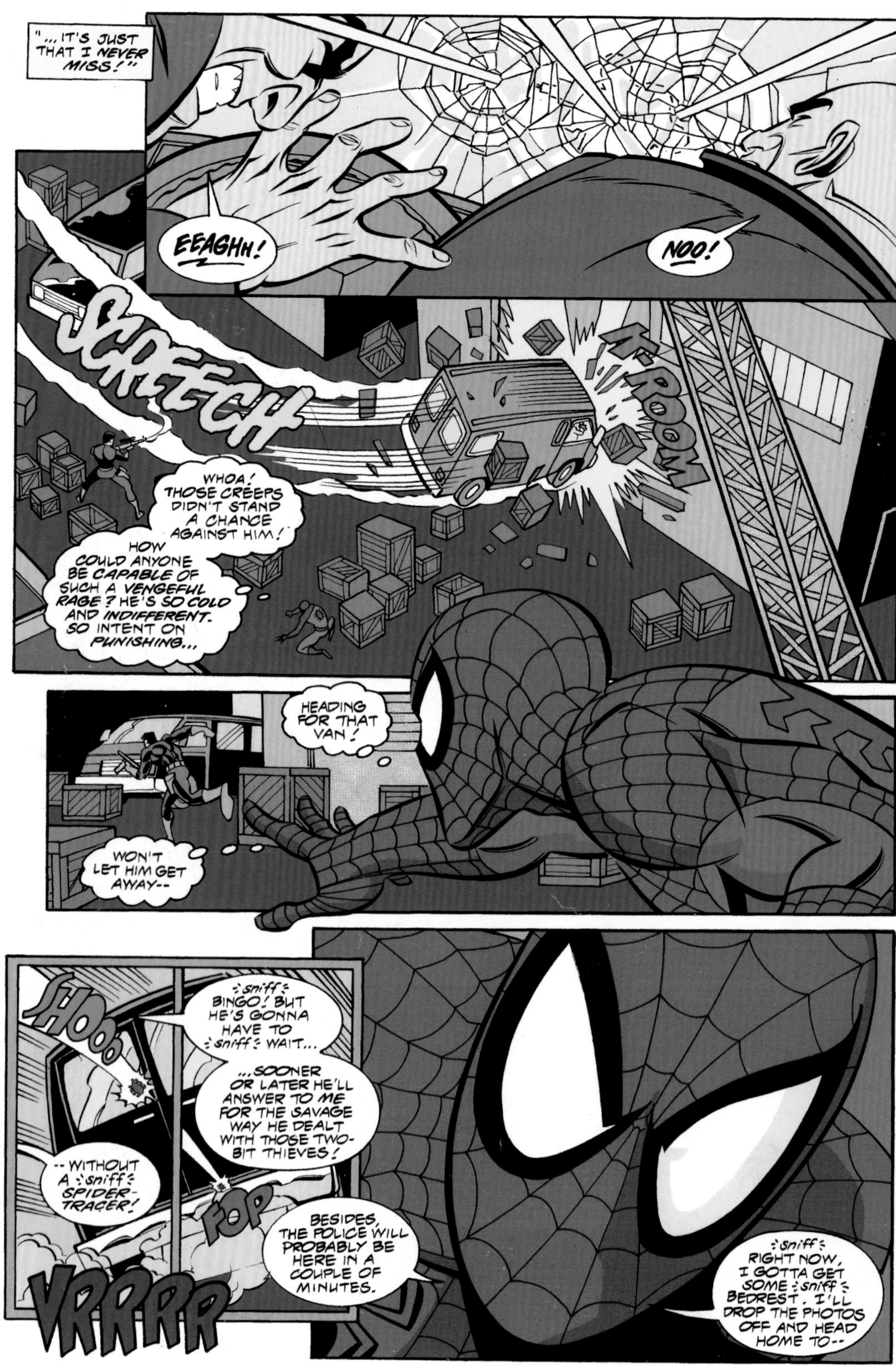
"...IT'S JUST THAT I NEVER MISS!"
EEAGHH!
NOO!
SCREECH
K-ROOM
WHOA! THOSE CREEPS DIDN'T STAND A CHANCE AGAINST HIM!
HOW COULD ANYONE BE CAPABLE OF SUCH A VENGEFUL RAGE? HE'S SO COLD AND INDIFFERENT. SO INTENT ON PUNISHING...
HEADING FOR THAT VAN!
WON'T LET HIM GET AWAY--
SHOOO
sniff BINGO! BUT HE'S GONNA HAVE TO sniff WAIT...
...SOONER OR LATER HE'LL ANSWER TO ME FOR THE SAVAGE WAY HE DEALT WITH THOSE TWO-BIT THIEVES!
--WITHOUT A sniff SPIDER-TRACER!
FOP
BESIDES, THE POLICE WILL PROBABLY BE HERE IN A COUPLE OF MINUTES.
VRRRRR
sniff RIGHT NOW, I GOTTA GET SOME sniff BEDREST. I'LL DROP THE PHOTOS OFF AND HEAD HOME TO--

"--FOREST HILLS!"
SO ⁝sniff⁝ I'M REALLY SORRY, AUNT MAY--
--BUT WITH THE WAY I FEEL, I JUST COULDN'T MAKE IT TO PICK UP YOUR NEW GLASSES.
I ⁝sniff⁝ PROMISE TO GET THEM FIRST THING TOMORROW.
YOU'LL DO NO SUCH THING, PETER. YOU'LL GET RID OF THAT AWFUL COLD BEFORE YOU PUT ONE FOOT OUT OF THIS HOUSE.
THEN WE CAN WORRY ABOUT THOSE GLASSES.
BESIDES, I'VE DONE WITHOUT THEM FOR SO LONG. A FEW MORE DAYS WON'T MATTER.
NOW AS FOR YOU, YOUNG MAN...
...YOU'RE GOING TO MARCH STRAIGHT UPSTAIRS AND GET INTO BED. I'LL CALL DR. ANDREANI.
⁝sniff⁝ B-BUT AUNT MAY, I'M REALLY NOT THAT ⁝achew⁝ SICK...
IS THAT SO? NOW YOU SCOOT. I'LL BE RIGHT UP WITH SOME HOT TEA AND HONEY. I KNOW HOW MUCH YOU LIKE THAT.
OKAY, AUNT MAY, I SHOULD KNOW ⁝sniff⁝ BETTER THAN TO ARGUE WITH YOU.
MAN, AM I LUCKY!
WHERE ELSE IN THIS TOWN AM I GONNA FIND HER KIND OF TENDER LOVING CARE?
STOP DAWDLING, DEAR, AND GO ON UPSTAIRS.
HAH! AUNT MAY, YOU'RE THE GREATEST!

LATER THAT EVENING, IN THE OFFICES OF THE PUBLISHER OF MANHATTAN'S MOST INFLUENTIAL NEWS-PAPER...
DAILY BUGLE
LOOK AT THIS! FINALLY! A CRIMEFIGHTER WHO ISN'T AFRAID TO DISH OUT REAL PUNISHMENT TO CRIMINALS!
MAYBE WE'VE SEEN THE LAST OF THOSE USELESS BLEEDING HEART SUPER HEROES!
THIS KIND OF HERO ON OUR FRONT PAGE SELLS NEWSPAPERS, TOO!
DON'T BE TOO QUICK TO ENDORSE THIS GUY, JJ. YOU DON'T KNOW ANYTHING ABOUT HIM EXCEPT THE SKETCHY POLICE REPORT--
DAILY BUGLE
VIGILANTE GUNMAN STOPS WATERFRONT THEFT!
--AND PETE'S PHOTOS.
YOU AFRAID TO TAKE ON THIS TOWN'S CRIMINAL SLIME, ROBBIE? WELL, I'LL TELL YA-- I'M NOT! AND NEITHER IS THE BUGLE!
THIS GUY AND HIS BIG GUNS ARE GONNA STOP CRIME IN NEW YORK--AND MY NEWSPAPER WILL BE RIGHT THERE TO HELP HIM!
I'M GOIN' HOME NOW, BUT DON'T FORGET THAT I'VE GOT TO LEAVE EARLY TOMORROW TO PICK UP THE NEW MERCEDES.
THE DEALER CALLED TODAY AND TOLD ME MY SPECIAL PLATES CAME IN. THEY READ, "JJ BUGLE". YA GET IT? PRETTY CLASSY, EH?
SEEYA IN THE MORNIN'!

MEANWHILE...
BREEP BREEP
MY SPIDER-TRACER BEEPER! IT FINALLY PICKED UP HIS VAN!
SNIFF COULDN'T GET HIM OUT OF MY MIND EVEN WHILE I WAS NAPPING!
SURE, HE BROKE UP THAT HEIST, BUT HE HURT THOSE GUYS PRETTY BAD. THAT'S NOT THE WAY A REAL CRIMEFIGHTER DOES BUSINESS.
NOT IN MY TOWN, ANYWAY...
...AND DEFINITELY NOT WHILE I'M AROUND!
PETER DEAR, ARE YOU ALL RIGHT?
OH NO! AUNT MAY MUST HAVE HEARD THE BEEPER! SHE'S COMING UP THE STAIRS!
SHE'S GONNA CATCH ME IN COSTUME! GOTTA THINK FAST!
I MUST'VE ACCIDENTALLY TURNED ON PETER'S ALARM CLOCK WHEN I WAS DUSTING TODAY!
I HOPE IT HASN'T WOKEN HIM...
OH, HE'S FINE. SLEEPING LIKE A LAMB UNDER HIS COVERS. THANK GOODNESS HE WASN'T DISTURBED.
I DON'T LIKE FOOLING AUNT MAY BY ROLLING UP MY SHEETS TO LOOK LIKE I'M UNDER THE COVERS, BUT I CAN'T EVER LET HER KNOW THAT I'M REALLY SPIDER-MAN...
LORD KNOWS WHAT THE SHOCK WOULD DO TO HER...

SOMEWHERE UNDER THE CRUMBLING ROADWAY OF THE WEST SIDE HIGHWAY...
KBLAM
KBLAM
KBLAM
HE'S FIGHTIN' LIKE A FREAKIN' ONE-MAN ARMY! DOES HE KNOW WHO HE'S MESSIN' WITH, MAN?
EEAAH!
BRATABRATA
BRATABRATA
I KNOW ALL I HAVE TO, PUNK! ALL ABOUT THE DRUG DEALS, THE MURDERS, THE FILTHY MONEY...
...ALL THE HORRORS YOU AND YOUR OVERLORDS DUMP ON INNOCENT PEOPLE!
IT'S ALL GONNA END-- STARTING HERE AND NOW!
HE AIN'T GONNA LET US OUTTA HERE ALIVE! WE SHOULDN'T BE MESSIN' WITH HIM!
SHUT UP AND LOOK! A FEW OF THE BOYS'VE SNUCK UP BEHIND HIM AND--
"--OH NO! IT'S SPIDER-MAN!"
SIX AGAINST ONE, EH? I'M NOT CRAZY ABOUT THE GUY IN THE BLACK TIGHTS, EITHER, BUT DON'T THOSE ODDS SEEM JUST A LITTLE LOPSIDED?
SPIDER-MAN. DIRTY SON-OF-A...

TELL YA WHAT... LET'S EVEN 'EM OUT.
I HEAR THE YANKEES MIGHT BE LOOKING FOR A NEW THIRD BASEMAN WHO CAN HIT WITH POWER.
YOU GUYS UP FOR SOME OFF-SEASON BATTING PRACTICE?
THEY DON'T PLAY BASEBALL WHERE YOU'RE GOING, WEB-MAN!
SHRING
SHOULD'VE KNOWN THAT WAS COMING! MY SPIDER-SENSE MUST BE MESSED UP REAL GOOD WITH THIS COLD!
ONLY ONE GUY COULD--
YOU'RE STICKING YOUR NOSE WHERE IT DOESN'T BELONG... AGAIN. I'M WARNIN' YOU, SPIDER-MAN-- STOP MESSING AROUND IN MY WAR!
GET OUTTA HERE BEFORE YOU END UP DEAD LIKE THESE GUYS'LL BE!
:sniff NO WAY, COWBOY! MURDER ISN'T THE WAY WE DEAL WITH CRIME IN THESE PARTS...
...NOW PUT THAT PIECE DOWN BEFORE I PUT IT WHERE THE SUN DOESN'T SHINE!
C'MON! LET'S GET THE HECK OUT OF HERE WHILE THEY'RE ARGUIN'!
LET THE BOSS KNOW WHAT HAPPENED! TELL 'IM THIS DEAL STILL GOES DOWN TONIGHT!

KISS YOUR BUTTS GOODBYE, SCUM...
...'CAUSE YOU'RE NEVER GONNA MAKE IT TO THAT VAN!
H-HEY--!

YOU GOT A :sniff: PROBLEM WITH YOUR HEARING, PAL?
I SAID, "PUT THE GUN DOWN"!
GET YOUR FREAKIN' HANDS OFF ME, SPIDER-MAN...

CHANK
OOMPH!
...I GOT A JOB TO FINISH!

I'VE BEEN TRACKING THIS DRUG CARTEL FROM SOUTH AMERICA TO NEW YORK OVER THE LAST SIX WEEKS--
--AND NO WIMPY SPANDEX GLAMOR-BOY WITH THE SNIFFLES IS GONNA STOP ME NOW!

THWIP
YOU'RE NOT GOIN' ANYWHERE, COWBOY! 'SPECIALLY AFTER THAT NASTY "GLAMOR BOY" REMARK!
FWAT

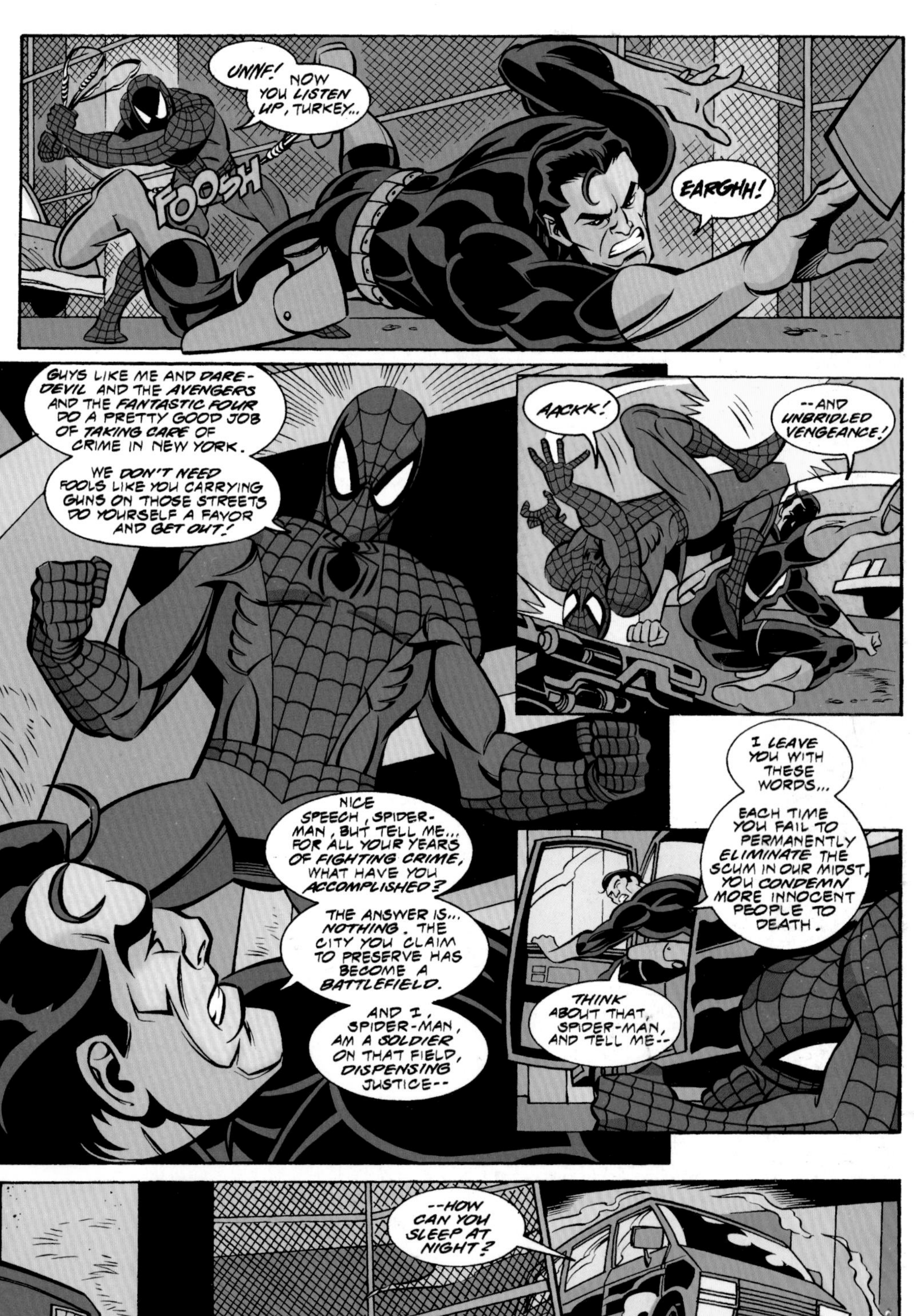
UNNF! NOW YOU LISTEN UP, TURKEY...
FOOSH
EARGHH!
GUYS LIKE ME AND DARE-DEVIL AND THE AVENGERS AND THE FANTASTIC FOUR DO A PRETTY GOOD JOB OF TAKING CARE OF CRIME IN NEW YORK.
WE DON'T NEED FOOLS LIKE YOU CARRYING GUNS ON THOSE STREETS DO YOURSELF A FAVOR AND GET OUT!
AACKK!
--AND UNBRIDLED VENGEANCE!
NICE SPEECH, SPIDER-MAN, BUT TELL ME... FOR ALL YOUR YEARS OF FIGHTING CRIME, WHAT HAVE YOU ACCOMPLISHED?
THE ANSWER IS... NOTHING. THE CITY YOU CLAIM TO PRESERVE HAS BECOME A BATTLEFIELD.
AND I, SPIDER-MAN, AM A SOLDIER ON THAT FIELD, DISPENSING JUSTICE--
I LEAVE YOU WITH THESE WORDS...
EACH TIME YOU FAIL TO PERMANENTLY ELIMINATE THE SCUM IN OUR MIDST, YOU CONDEMN MORE INNOCENT PEOPLE TO DEATH.
THINK ABOUT THAT, SPIDER-MAN, AND TELL ME--
--HOW CAN YOU SLEEP AT NIGHT?

YOU AND ME ARE GONNA HAVE PLENTY OF TIME TO DISCUSS THOSE PEARLS OF WISDOM, STRANGER, 'CAUSE FROM HERE ON IN--
FWAT
THWIP
--WE'RE GONNA BE OOMPH INSEPARABLE!
SPIDER-MAN! YOU DON'T GET IT, DO YOU?
YOUR INTERFERENCE IN MY WORK MAKES YOU AS GUILTY AS THOSE DEATH-DEALIN', DRUG-PUSHIN' SLIMEBALLS!
AND YOU'RE GONNA PAY THE SAME PRICE THEY WILL!
SCREEEE
GOTTA HANG ON! GOTTA STOP HIM--
--BEFORE HE HAS A CHANCE TO KILL THOSE PUNKS!

YOU AGAIN ?! WHAT THE @#$% DO YOU WANT FROM ME ?
sniff UH, LET ME THINK... A SPARE KLEENEX PERHAPS ?
OR HOW 'BOUT JUST HEARING ME OUT...?
MERCEDES-B
NEW

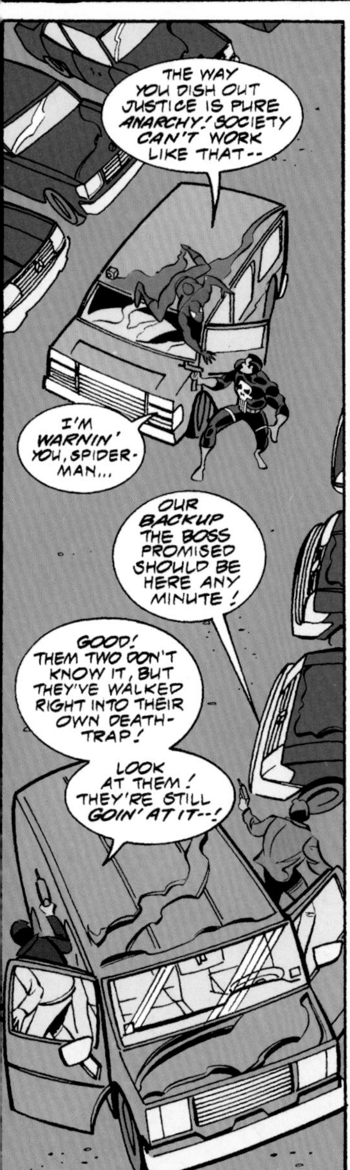
THE WAY YOU DISH OUT JUSTICE IS PURE ANARCHY! SOCIETY CAN'T WORK LIKE THAT--
I'M WARNIN' YOU, SPIDER-MAN...
OUR BACKUP THE BOSS PROMISED SHOULD BE HERE ANY MINUTE !
GOOD! THEM TWO DON'T KNOW IT, BUT THEY'VE WALKED RIGHT INTO THEIR OWN DEATH-TRAP!
LOOK AT THEM ! THEY'RE STILL GOIN' AT IT--!

FWAT
NO, FOOL, I'M WARNIN' YOU! NO MAN IN THIS WORLD HAS THE RIGHT TO BE JUDGE, JURY AND EXECUTIONER FOR SOMEONE HE THINKS IS GUILTY!
AND NO MAN HAS THE RIGHT TO PREVENT ME FROM PROTECTING THE INNOCENT AND LAW-ABIDING--
EARRGH!
JJ BUG

NOT ONLY DO I HAVE THE RIGHT, BUT I HAVE THE RESPONSIBILITY TO STOP YOU FROM MURDERING!

SAVE YOUR BREATH, HERO..

"... THE CHOIRBOYS JUST ARRIVED!

" AND THEY'RE NOT IN THE MOOD FOR ANY SERMONS!"

THOSE BOYS ARE THE ELITE HIT SQUAD OF THE SYNDICATE I TOLD YOU ABOUT. MURDER IS THEIR WAY OF LIFE.

SO UNLESS YOU WANNA STAY PUT FOR TARGET PRACTICE, WE BETTER PUT OUR DIFFERENCES ASIDE AND--

AGREED, BUT WE PLAY--

SPLAM
SPLAM
WHO THE @#$% DO YOU THINK YOU--
GUNFIRE! GET DOWN!
GAACK I WILL AS SOON AS I CAN START GAACK BREATHING AGAIN...
HAVING THESE GUYS RUN AWAY WHILE WE FIGHT IS GETTING TO BE A BAD HABIT, COWBOY...!
NOW THEY'RE IN THAT BRAND-NEW MERCEDES!
BLAM
BLAM
BLAM
BLAM
JJBUGLE
YOUR WAY FAILED, SPIDER-MAN! TIME TO DO IT MY WAY...
...AND THAT'S BY ANY MEANS NECESSARY!
SHRAKA
SHRAKA
PWAM!
SHRANG
SHRANG
SHRANG
KRAMM
I REST MY CASE.

YOU'RE LUCKY. THEY'RE STILL ALIVE.
THE COPS AND MEDICAL EMERGENCY TEAM WILL BE HERE SOON TO TAKE CARE OF THEM.
YOU, MY TRIGGER-HAPPY FRIEND, ARE GONNA HAVE A LOT OF QUESTIONS TO ANSWER.
I'M OUTTA HERE. MY WORK'S DONE ANYWAY.
EVEN I WOULDN'T KILL THESE POOR SLOBS IN THE CONDITION THEY'RE IN...
BUT WE BOTH KNOW THEY'LL BE OUT ON THE STREETS IN NO TIME...
...AND THAT'S WHEN I NAIL THEM...
...BECAUSE YOU CAN'T BE EVERYWHERE TO STOP ME.
DON'T COUNT ON IT, COWBOY. YOU'LL BE SURPRISED HOW I POP UP IN THE DARNDEST PLACES.
GET OUT OF HERE. NOW.
JUST KEEP THINKING ABOUT WHAT I'VE BEEN SAYIN' TO YOU. SOMEDAY IT'LL ALL MAKE SENSE.
ONE MORE THING, COWBOY. WHAT'S YOUR NAME?
THE PUNISHER. THAT'S ALL YOU NEED TO KNOW.
ADIOS.
SORRY TO DISAPPOINT YOU, PUNISHER... BUT IT'LL NEVER MAKE SENSE TO ME.

THE NEXT DAY...
THESE ARE TERRIFIC, PETE...!
DAILY BUGLE
GREAT PICS! I DON'T KNOW HOW YOU DO IT!
sniff THANKS, ROBBIE. I CAN'T WAIT TO SEE WHAT JONAH THINKS ABOUT THEM!
FEAST YOUR EYES ON SPIDER-MAN TAKING DOWN A BUNCH OF HOODS AT A CAR DEALERSHIP LAST NIGHT!
PETE GOT IT ALL ON FILM!
SAVE THE REVIEWS, ROBBIE! LEMME SEE THOSE!
UH, HI, JJ...
IT WAS THAT VIGILANTE PAL OF YOURS THAT DEMOLISHED THE NEW CAR. BOY, DOES HE GET AROUND!
HMMM, THOSE PLATES... THOSE LICENSE PLATES! OH, MY GOD--!
THAT'S MY CAR! MY BRAND-NEW $50,000 MERCEDES!
LOOK WHAT SPIDER-MAN AND THAT LUNATIC DID TO MY CAR, ROBBIE!
WHO DO THESE VIGILANTES THINK THEY ARE, DESTROYING INNOCENT PEOPLE'S PROPERTY?
ARRGH! GET OUT OF HERE--THE BOTH OF YOU! I WANT TO BE ALONE!
I WAS JUST LEAVING, JJ...
...TO HEAD OUT TO QUEENS AND FINALLY PICK UP AUNT MAY'S GLASSES...

sniff I JUST DON'T UNDERSTAND IT, AUNT MAY...
...BUT WHEN I GOT TO THE EYEGLASS STORE TO PICK UP YOUR NEW GLASSES, HE LOOKED AT ME AS IF I WAS CRAZY!
EYEGLASS STORE? BUT, PETER--
--WHY WOULD YOU GO TO AN EYEGLASS STORE--
--TO PICK UP MY NEW DRINKING GLASSES?
I HAVE PERFECT EYESIGHT. YOU SHOULD KNOW THAT, DEAR.
B-BUT WHEN YOU SAID "GLASSES" I THOUGHT YOU MEANT--
I KNEW YOU WEREN'T FEELING WELL, SO I PICKED THEM UP MYSELF THIS MORNING.
THAT COLD IS REALLY CLOUDING UP YOUR HEAD, PETER.
C'MON, YOUNG MAN, UP TO BED WITH YOU...
sniff FOR GOODNESS SAKE, AUNT MAY, THIS ISN'T NECESSARY...
...IS IT?
OH, WHAT'S THE USE? HERE WE GO AGAIN...!
NEXT ISSUE:
HAMMERHEAD STRIKES

MARVEL COMICS
NEW STORIES BASED ON THE HIT TV SHOW!
APPROVED BY THE COMICS CODE AUTHORITY
THE ADVENTURES OF SPIDER-MAN
SPIDER-MAN
MAY '96 2
ONLY 99¢
SAVIUK & STULL
HAMMERHEAD STRIKES!

NEL YOMTOV WRITER | ALEX SAVIUK PENCILER | ROB STULL INKER | STEVE DUTRO LETTERER | KEVIN TINSLEY COLORIST | MOSSOFF & POWERS EDITORS | BOB HARRAS CHIEF

--ALLEY OOPS!--
--OF THE HOME COURT!
C'MON, BOYS, LET'S SEE WHAT YOU'VE GOT!
AS IF I DON'T KNOW ENOUGH ABOUT THEM ALREADY...

"KINGPIN IS 450 POUNDS OF ROCK-SOLID MUSCLE. HIS SCALY FRIEND, THE LIZARD...
"...CAN SNAP MY SPINE WITH ONE FLICK OF HIS TAIL!"

UN-FORTUNATELY, IT HAPPENS TO BE THAT HE'S REALLY CURT CONNORS...
...MY GOOD FRIEND AND COLLEGE PROFESSOR!
COMING UP FAST--!

"THE RHINO!"
"A HUMAN BATTERING RAM WITH THE INTELLIGENCE OF A SLUG...
"...BUT ONE THAT CAN BENCH-PRESS 80 TONS!"

NEED SOME SPACE TO OPERATE... I'LL TRY TO LURE THEM OUT ONE OF THE UPSTAIRS WINDOWS!
JUST HOPE WE DON'T MUSS UP AUNT MAY'S SEWING ROOM!
UH-OH!

"DR. OCTOPUS!
"HERE'S WHAT HAPPENS WHEN YOU CROSS A DEMENTED SCIENTIST WITH 8 TITANIUM TENTACLES THAT SHRED, CRUSH, SPLICE AND DICE!"

BLOCKING MY WAY... VENOM!
HOW AM I GONNA GET PAST HIM?

"EVERY BIT MY EQUAL AND MAYBE MORE, THE ALIEN SYMBIOTE OF THAT COSTUME ONCE POSSESSED ME...
"... ALMOST MAKING ME A HOMICIDAL KILLER!"

NO! OUT OF WEB FLUID! WHAT A TIME FOR MY CARTRIDGES TO GO DRY!
TIME TO GET THE HECK OUT OF HERE-- WHILE I STILL HAVE MY LIFE!

YOU! I SHOULD'VE KNOWN THIS LYNCH MOB WOULDN'T BE COMPLETE WITHOUT--

--KRAVEN THE HUNTER!
YOU HAVE YOUR CHOICE, JUNGLE BOY: YOU CAN EITHER STEP ASIDE OR STAND THERE LIKE AN IDIOT--

--WHILE I GO OVER YOU!
BESIDES, THERE'S NO CREATURE ON EARTH AS DETERMINED AS A PARKER ON THE WAY TO THE--

--KITCHEN! WHOOAAAAa
KRASH
BRANNK
GREAT GOING, SPIDEY! SO WHEN DID YOU START MOON-LIGHTING AS A ONE-MAN WRECKING CREW?
THIS WAS KRAVEN'S FAULT...
HEY, FURBOY! YOU MADE ME BREAK THAT FAUCET! NOW I'M GONNA BREAK YOU!
YOU'RE GONNA LEARN THE HARD WAY THAT I'M NO EASY...
...PUSHOVER!
POOSH
AH, I WAS GETTING TIRED OF THE SILENT TREATMENT YOU GUYS WERE GIVING ME, ANYWAY!
FUNTIME'S OVER. BETTER FIND A WRENCH AND FIX THAT THING PRONTO...
I BET THE AVENGERS DON'T HAVE TO WORRY ABOUT WRECKING THE PLUMBING WHEN THEY TRAIN!

WHILE SPIDEY READIES FOR HIS ROLE AS MR. HOME IMPROVEMENT...
DAILY BUGLE
...SO USE YOUR HEAD AND DO WHAT I SAY...
...OR YOU WON'T LIVE TO SEE ANOTHER EDITION OF THIS RAG GO TO PRESS!

YOU LISTEN UP, MISTER.
FOR THE LAST TIME... STOP RUNNIN' THESE ANTI-CRIME EDITORIALS OF YOURS.
OR ELSE.
DON'T THINK YOU'LL BE THE ONLY ONE AROUND HERE WHO GETS HURT, ROBERTSON. I PROMISE YOU-- THERE'LL BE OTHERS.

I-I'M NOT AFRAID OF YOUR THREATS!
YOU'RE TALKING TO THE EDITOR IN CHIEF OF THIS CITY'S MOST INFLUENTIAL PAPER...
...AND I DON'T SCARE EASILY.
AND BESIDES...

JUST WHO IN BLAZES DO YOU AND THESE GOONS THINK YOU ARE BARGING INTO MY OFFICE--
I WONDERED WHEN YOU WAS GONNA ASK ME THAT, NEWSBOY...

BUGLE
E-BOSS IN JAIL
BUGLE
DER-MAN
R-VILLAIN
THE NAME... IS
HAMMERHEAD!
NOT A MONICKER YOU'RE GONNA FORGET REAL EASY!
DAI
SPID
ME
AND NOW THAT YOU KNOW WHO I AM, OUR BUSINESS TOGETHER IS FINISHED. I'M GONNA GIVE YOU SOME PERSONAL SPACE TO THINK ABOUT OUR CONVERSATION.
I GOT A FEELIN' YOU'LL MAKE THE SMART DECISION...

"I'M NO TIM ALLEN, BUT FIXING THAT FAUCET WAS CHILD'S PLAY!
DAILY BUGLE
"AND IT'S A GOOD THING IT WAS. ROBBIE HATES IT WHEN PEOPLE SHOW UP LATE FOR APPOINTMENTS...
GET A LOAD OF THOSE GUYS! THEY LOOK LIKE EXTRAS STRAIGHT OUT OF AN OLD EDWARD G. ROBINSON MOVIE...!
IT'S NOT HALLOWEEN AND I'LL BET THEY'RE NOT THE NEW REPORTERS FOR THE BUGLE'S SOCIETY PAGE, SO I WONDER...
...WHAT ARE THEY DOING HERE?
COULD THEY HAVE ANYTHING TO DO WITH THE RECENT SERIES OF GANGLAND CRIME PIECES WE'VE BEEN RUNNING?
HMM, MAYBE ROBBIE KNOWS SOMETHING ABOUT THEM...
...SO KILL MY EDITORIAL ON MOB INVOLVEMENT AT THE CONVENTION CENTER, DAVE.
I'LL WORK UP A MORE UPBEAT PIECE AND HAVE IT DOWN TO YOU IN THIRTY MINUTES.
WHAT?! ROBBIE'S KILLING ONE OF HIS PIECES? HE'S NEVER DONE THAT BEFORE!
WHAT'S THIS ALL ABOUT?

HEY, ROBBIE, WHAT GIVES?
YOU HEARD RIGHT, PETE. THREE GUYS JUST THREATENED TO KILL ME AND SOME OTHER PEOPLE AROUND HERE IF I DON'T STOP THE EDITORIALS...
I DIDN'T MEAN TO EAVESDROP, BUT DID I HEAR YOU RIGHT? YOU'RE GONNA PULL ONE OF YOUR PIECES?
YOU MUST'VE PASSED THEM IN THE HALL...
THE BIG ONE CALLS HIMSELF HAMMERHEAD... AND HE MEANS BUSINESS.
DAILY BUGLE
NEWS TIP HELPS POLICE ARREST KIDNAPPER
CRIME BOSS NOW IN JAIL
IF HIS GANG IS WHAT I THINK IT IS, THEY'VE BECOME THE BIGGEST AND MOST FEARED CRIME SYNDICATE IN NEW YORK CITY.
I'LL TELL YA KID, I'VE SEEN ALL KINDS OF THINGS IN THIRTY YEARS ON THE JOB.
BUT THIS... THIS HAS ME SCARED.
THEN YOU GOTTA TELL JAMESON. YOU SHOULDN'T HAVE TO--
NO. HE'LL BE BACK IN A COUPLE OF DAYS. I CAN'T GO RUNNING TO HIM EVERY TIME A PROBLEM POPS UP AROUND HERE.
I WON'T RUN THIS PIECE IN TONIGHT'S EDITION AND RISK ANYTHING BAD HAPPENING TO OUR PEOPLE. I JUST WON'T.
WHAT? YOU'VE ALWAYS TOLD ME THIS PAPER HAD A RESPONSIBILITY TO PROTECT THE PUBLIC INTEREST!
DOING THAT IS THE RIGHT THING! AND THE RIGHT THING NOW IS TO TAKE A STAND AGAINST THOSE BUMS!
I MUST BE GETTING SOFT IN MY OLD AGE...
YOU'RE RIGHT, OF COURSE. THE PIECE RUNS TONIGHT AS PLANNED!
AND THERE'LL BE MORE TO FOLLOW. THANKS, PETE!
WAY TO GO, ROBBIE! I'M PROUD OF YOU! I PROMISE YOU WON'T REGRET IT...!

THE NEXT MORNING...
MAN! ROBBIE REALLY HIT A HOME RUN WITH LAST NIGHT'S EDITORIAL...
THE AUTHORITIES ARE GONNA JUMP ON HIS PIECE AND RUN THAT MOB OUT OF NEW YORK IN NO TIME!
IF I WAS HAMMERHEAD, I'D PACK MY BAGS, BUY A BUS TICKET AS LONG AS MY ARM AND GET THE HECK OUT OF HERE!
DAILY BUGLE
CONVENTION CENTER RUN BY MOB
NOW... JUST A COUPLE OF MORE TWISTS ON THIS PIPE AND I'LL HAVE THIS FAUCET WORKING LIKE NEW...
RINNNG
OKAY, I'LL BE RIGHT THERE--!
KONK
OWW! WHAT A TIME FOR A PHONE CALL!
MR. ROBERTSON'S BEEN HOSPITALIZED, PETER! HE WAS FOUND BEATEN AT HIS APARTMENT LAST NIGHT!
I'VE CALLED MR. JAMESON... HE'S COMING RIGHT BACK TO NEW YORK. I THOUGHT YOU SHOULD KNOW--
D-DON'T WORRY, EDNA. I-I'M SURE ROBBIE WILL BE ALL RIGHT.
TH-THANKS FOR CALLING. I'LL SEE YA...
OH, NO! THIS IS MY FAULT!
IF I HADN'T OPENED MY BIG MOUTH, ROBBIE WOULD BE ALL RIGHT!
I'VE GOT TO GO SEE HIM... MAKE SURE HE'S OKAY.

THE LINDSAY CONVENTION CENTER...
...SO I HEAR YOU GUYS HAVE A PROBLEM WITH OUR ARRANGEMENTS...
YOU WANTED TO SPEAK FOR THE GROUP, MISTA NATHAN?
GREEN'S COMICON THIS WEEKEND ALL WELC
GREEN'D COMIC CON
M-MR. HAMMERHEAD... WHEN YOU TOLD ME I HAD TO BUY MY CONCESSION STAND SUPPLIES FROM YOU, I DIDN'T MIND...
--BUT YOU RAISED YOUR PRICES TOO HIGH.
I-I CAN'T AFFORD TO STAY IN BUSINESS ANYMORE...
J-JOSEPHS CAN'T EVEN HAVE THE CENTER CLEANED AFTER A SHOW BECAUSE YOUR JANITOR SERVICE IS TOO EXPENSIVE...
I SEE. GO ON, NATHAN...
THE ALLENS HAD TO PAY YOUR ELECTRICIAN FIFTY DOLLARS JUST TO CHANGE A LIGHT BULB...
W-WE CAN'T LIVE LIKE THIS. TH-THINGS HAVE GOT TO CH-CHANGE...
YOU WANT CHANGE, NATHAN? I'LL TELL YA WHAT...
FROM NOW ON--
--YOU PAY TWICE AS MUCH!
WE HAD A DEAL, SCUM! YOU AGREED TO BUY MY SERVICES, MY SUPPLIES, AND MY PROTECTION!
AND YOU'RE GONNA PAY MY PRICES--NO MATTER HOW HIGH THEY BECOME!

DAILY BUGLE
CONVENTION CENTER RUN BY MOB
AND DON'T GET ANY IDEAS ABOUT BABBLING TO THE COPS ABOUT THIS! I'LL KILL ANY ONE OF YOU WHO OPENS UP HIS BIG MOUTH!
NOW GET OUT OF HERE, BUT REMEMBER...
...I WANNA SEE SMILES ON ALL YOUR FACES FOR THE COMIC BOOK KIDS THIS WEEKEND!
HA HA HA HA!
GOOD GOIN', HAMMERHEAD. YOU CLAMMED THEM UP FAST. WORD'S GETTIN' OUT NOT TO MESS WITH YOU!
'SPECIALLY AFTER YOUR WORK LAST NIGHT, SPIDER...
TOO BAD ROBERTSON DIDN'T TAKE MY ADVICE. HE'S LEARNED HIS LESSON, THOUGH.
NOW NOBODY'S GONNA BE STUPID ENOUGH TO TAKE ME ON. Y'KNOW, BOYS, IT'S JUST A MATTER OF TIME--
Green's COMIKON THIS WEEKEND ALL WELCOME!
--BEFORE I HAVE THIS CITY ON ITS KNEES BEFORE ME!
N TION
R RULED
OB!
CONVE
NTE

...I CAN'T BELIEVE THIS HAS HAPPENED! I WANT ONE GOOD REASON--
MERCY HOSPITAL
--WHY YOU DID SOMETHING SO STUPID!
MAYBE NOW ISN'T THE TIME FOR THIS, MR. JAMESON. ROBBIE'S HURTIN' REAL BAD--
HOLD ON, PETE. JONAH OWNS THE BUGLE. HE DESERVES AN ANSWER.
HAMMER-HEAD'S INTO BIG-TIME EXTORTION, DRUG-RUNNING, MURDER... YOU NAME IT, JONAH.
HE HAS TO BE SHUT DOWN AND PUT AWAY--AND THE BUGLE HAS TO HELP DO IT.
I HOPE YOU CAN SEE WHY I MADE THIS DECISION.
BESIDES, PETE AND I TALKED AND WE BOTH FELT IT WAS THE RIGHT THING TO DO--
OH, YOU DID, eh?
WELL, I'M THE BOSS, ROBBIE, AND I HAVE THE RIGHT TO KNOW WHAT HAPPENS IN MY ABSENCE!
YOU SHOULD'VE TOLD ME WHAT WAS GOING ON!
SORRY IF I MESSED UP, JONAH--
F-FORGET IT, ROBBIE. FOR ONCE, PARKER'S RIGHT-- NOW ISN'T THE TIME FOR THIS. WE'LL LEAVE...
ONE MORE THING... IF YOU WERE IN MY SHOES, I'D BET YOU WOULD'VE RUN THE EDITORIAL, RIGHT?
I'D LIKE TO THINK SO, ROBBIE. C'MON, PARKER, LET'S GO...

PARKER! WHERE IN BLAZES DO YOU THINK YOU'RE RUNNING OFF TO?
I WANT A FEW WORDS WITH YOU, BOY!
WHAT DID ROBBIE MEAN WHEN HE SAID YOU "TALKED" TO HIM ABOUT DOING THE "RIGHT THING"?
DID YOU PUT ROBBIE UP TO RUNNING THAT EDITORIAL EVEN AFTER HAMMERHEAD'S THREATS?
B-BUT, JONAH, WE CAN'T GIVE IN TO--
WHERE DO YOU COME OFF MAKING THAT KIND OF EXECUTIVE DECISION?
YOU'RE THE ONE RESPONSIBLE FOR WHAT HAPPENED TO ROBBIE!
NEXT TIME KEEP YOUR MOUTH SHUT AND LET GROWN MEN LIKE ME RUN MY BUSINESS!
WHILE YOU'RE AT IT, CHEW ON THIS, BONEHEAD...
...WITH ROBBIE HELPLESSLY LYING IN PAIN, WHAT KIND OF ADVICE DO YOU HAVE FOR HIM NOW?
HE'S RIGHT. I CAN'T DO ANYTHING TO CHANGE WHAT'S ALREADY HAPPENED--
--BUT MAYBE I CAN MAKE UP FOR IT BY TAKING ON HAMMERHEAD AND FINISHING WHAT ROBBIE STARTED!

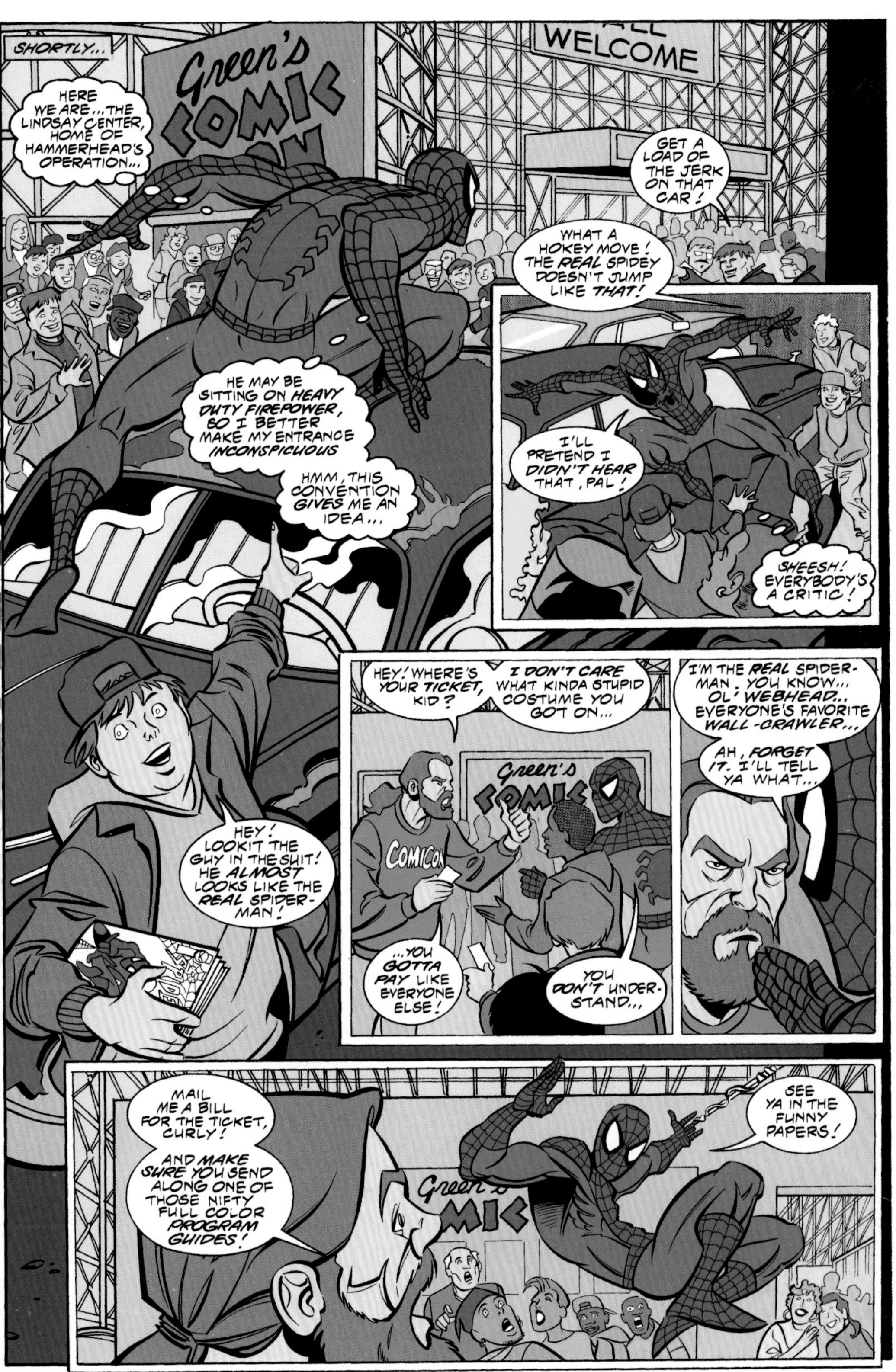

SHORTLY...
Green's COMIC
WELCOME
HERE WE ARE... THE LINDSAY CENTER, HOME OF HAMMERHEAD'S OPERATION...
GET A LOAD OF THE JERK ON THAT CAR!
WHAT A HOKEY MOVE! THE REAL SPIDEY DOESN'T JUMP LIKE THAT!
HE MAY BE SITTING ON HEAVY DUTY FIREPOWER, SO I BETTER MAKE MY ENTRANCE INCONSPICUOUS
HMM, THIS CONVENTION GIVES ME AN IDEA...
I'LL PRETEND I DIDN'T HEAR THAT, PAL!
SHEESH! EVERYBODY'S A CRITIC!
HEY! LOOKIT THE GUY IN THE SUIT! HE ALMOST LOOKS LIKE THE REAL SPIDER-MAN!
HEY! WHERE'S YOUR TICKET, KID?
I DON'T CARE WHAT KINDA STUPID COSTUME YOU GOT ON...
...YOU GOTTA PAY LIKE EVERYONE ELSE!
COMICON
Green's COMIC
YOU DON'T UNDER-STAND...
I'M THE REAL SPIDER-MAN. YOU KNOW... OL' WEBHEAD... EVERYONE'S FAVORITE WALL-CRAWLER...
AH, FORGET IT. I'LL TELL YA WHAT...
MAIL ME A BILL FOR THE TICKET, CURLY!
AND MAKE SURE YOU SEND ALONG ONE OF THOSE NIFTY FULL COLOR PROGRAM GUIDES!
SEE YA IN THE FUNNY PAPERS!

NICE "INCONSPICUOUS" ENTRANCE, SPIDEY! THE WHOLE PLACE HAS NOTICED ME!
JUST HOPE I CAN STILL GET THE DROP ON HAMMERHEAD...
UH-OH. TOO LATE.
THAT'S THEM DOWN THERE...
SPIDER-MAN! MOW 'IM DOWN, BOYS!
NOW!
SMASH!
THESE PUNKS GOTTA LEARN THAT I'M THE NEW LAW IN THIS TOWN!
ANYBODY THAT MESSES WIT' ME IS GONNA PAY!
AARRGH!
SPIDER-SENSE GOIN' WILD!
OH NO!
BRATTABRATTA
FWIT
BRATTABRATTABRAT

OH NO!
MY ORIGINAL ART! MY VINTAGE COMICS! YOU'VE RUINED ME!
OOMPH!
CRAMMCH
COOOL! I WONDER IF HE'LL SIGN MY ADVENTURES OF SPIDER-MAN #1!
KEEP THE CAP ON YOUR PEN, BUDDY-- I'M KINDA BUSY RIGHT NOW!
HAMMERHEAD'S TAKIN' OFF!
GOOD! THAT'LL TAKE THIS FIGHT OUT OF HERE...
...AWAY FROM ALL THESE INNOCENT FOLKS!
EXIT
I'LL TAKE THE DIRECT APPROACH AND HEAD THEM OFF IN THIS STAIRWELL!
OL' HAMMERHEAD AND HIS GOONS ARE SURE GONNA BE--
TRASH

SURPRISED? DON'T BE.
I BEEN HOPIN' FOR A COZY MEETING LIKE THIS FOR A LONG TIME.
SPARE ME THE PLEASANTRIES, HAMMERHEAD. I HAVEN'T COME TO TAKE TEA WITH YOU. I AM HERE--
--TO PAY YOU BACK AND SHUT YOU DOWN!
STUPID MOVE, SPIDER-MAN!
THAT'S NOT WHAT I CALL--
--USIN' YOUR HEAD!
KRUNG!
YAARGHH!
I BEEN TOLD THAT MY SKULL IS MADE OF SOLID STEEL.
I AIN'T COMPLAININ', MIND YA...
FWACK
...IT DOES GET THE JOB DONE.
SH-WROOM
KRROOM
BURIED! NO WAY HE GETS OUT ALIVE...!

OUTSIDE THE CONVENTION CENTER...
...PROBLEM IS THAT EVERYONE'S *AFRAID* TO TAKE THESE GANGSTERS ON *FACE-TO FACE!*
...EVERYONE EXCEPT *J. JONAH JAMESON!*
I DON'T CARE *HOW* TOUGH THEY'RE SUPPOSED TO BE...
I'LL TEACH THIS SCUM NOT TO MESS WITH ANYONE FROM *MY* PAPER!

SCREEE
SPIDER-MAN'S DEAD!
ONCE THE COPS GET WIND OF *THAT,* THEY'LL BE *DOWN* HERE LIKE A PACK OF HYENAS!
C'MON! WE'LL HEAD UPTOWN AND LAY *LOW* FOR A WHILE...
HMMF! THAT OLD TANK IS PARKED AT A METER WITH NO TIME LEFT ON IT...
...I'M GOING TO SPEAK TO SOMEONE ABOUT THIS!
HEY, BOSS, THAT'S *JAMESON...* FROM THE *BUGLE!*
PERFECT! WHY DON'T YOU BOYS GO *INTRODUCE* YOURSELVES...

...AND WHILE YOU'RE AT IT, GIVE 'IM *MY* REGARDS!
FWACK
JUST FOLLOWIN' ORDERS, JAMESON... DON'T TAKE IT PERSONALLY!
N-OOOWW! GAACK!

UNNH! TOOK ALMOST ALL MY STRENGTH TO GET FREE... MY HEAD... POUNDING LIKE A JACKHAMMER...
...BUT WHERE DID HAMMERHEAD--?
OH NO!
C'MON, REY! OUT HERE! A FIGHT!
THAT'S... JAMESON! WHAT'S HE DOING HERE?
JUST WHAT I NEEDED... ANOTHER HEADACHE!
WHACK
WHACK
WHACK
WELL, HERE WE GO AGAIN...
OHH... WHAT HIT ME...?
YEARGH!
THWIP
AMPFF!
JONAH'S HURT REAL BAD!
GOTTA TAKE OUT THESE TWO FAST--
--AND SEE IF HE'S STILL ALIVE!
HE'S BARELY BREATHING! HE NEEDS MEDICAL HELP-- NOW!
HANG IN, JJ! DON'T QUIT ON ME... PLEASE.
W-WHAT'S THAT?
NO...

KRRRRRRRR
HE'S OUTTA HIS EVER-LOVIN' MIND! WE'RE GONNA BE ROADKILL!
I'VE GOT NOWHERE TO GO!
UNLESS I MAKE LIKE MY OL' PAL THE HULK...
...AND TAKE THE FRIENDLY SKIES!
NICE MOVE PUNK, BUT CARRYIN' HIM AROUND IS GONNA MAKE YOU RUN OUT OF GAS A LOT SOONER THAN THIS CAR...
KRRR
...AND WHEN YOU DO...
...I'LL SMEAR YOU TWO ALL OVER THE STREET!
HE'S RIGHT, BUT I GOTTA PROTECT JJ AT ALL COSTS!
OKAY, FLATTOP IT'S SHOW-TIME...
...LET'S ROCK!
VRRRR

RATA TATATA
A TOMMY GUN? THOSE THINGS WENT OUT OF STYLE SIXTY YEARS AGO, HAMMERHEAD!
I'M SURPRISED YOU'RE NOT SHOOTING AT ME WITH A BLUNDERBUSS!
RATA TATATA
THIS IS MY LAST SHOT TO DERAIL HIM... GOTTA TIME MY JUMP PERFECTLY...
FORGET HOW OLD IT IS, PUNK! IT'S STILL GONNA RIP THROUGH YA LIKE A HOWITZER!
VRRRR
NOW!
PERFECT!
SHRAKK
SCREEE
KNOCKED HIM AWAY FROM JJ! THE QUESTION IS...
...WILL HAMMERHEAD COME BACK FOR MORE?
SCREEEE
GOOD... HE'S LEAVING. FINALLY.
I'LL NAIL HIM YET. RIGHT NOW, I'M STAYING HERE TO MAKE SURE THAT JONAH GETS TO A HOSPITAL...
VRRRR
...IF IT'S NOT TOO LATE.

...AND HIS OPERATION AT THE CONVENTION CENTER IS FINISHED

I HEARD THAT NATHAN AND THE OTHER CONCESSIONAIRES HAVE AGREED TO COOPERATE WITH THE POLICE.

ONCE HAMMERHEAD IS TRACKED DOWN, THERE'LL BE AN AVALANCHE OF EVIDENCE TO PUT HIM AWAY FOR A LONG TIME.

DON'T FORGET TO TAKE SOME CREDIT YOURSELF, PETE...

BETWEEN YOU URGING ME TO RUN MY PIECE AND SPIDER-MAN SHOWING UP--

SPIDER-MAN?!

FOREST HILLS, QUEENS...
...SHE'S AS GOOD AS NEW, SON...
...BUT IT'S GONNA COST YA $200. HAD TO REPLACE THE WHOLE PIPE.
TWO HUNDRED? I MUST BE IN THE WRONG BUSINESS...
...IT TAKES ME THREE WEEKS TO MAKES THIS KIND OF MONEY!
ED'S PLUMBING
PLEASE SEE YOURSELF OUT, ED.

...MY AUNT MAY WILL BE COMING HOME IN A COUPLE OF HOURS AND I'VE GOT TO CLEAN UP.
WHAT A RELAXING VACATION. I DIDN'T EVEN WORRY ABOUT PETER.
HE'S BECOME SUCH A MATURE RESPONSIBLE YOUNG MAN...
...I WONDER HOW THE SWEET DEAR IS.

A-AUNT MAY! BUT I WASN'T EXPECTING--
W-WHY DON'T YOU COME BACK LATER--
STOP YOUR TEASING, DEAR. STEP ASIDE AND LET ME COME IN.
O-OKAY... IF YOU INSIST...

OH NO! WHAT HAPPENED, PETER? DID I LEAVE A FAUCET RUNNING--?
NO. JUST A LITTLE ACCIDENT I HAD, AUNT MAY. SORRY.
YOU GO RELAX WHILE I CLEAN UP THE MESS AND THEN WE'LL HAVE A CUP OF TEA TOGETHER.

AFTER THAT, YOU CAN GIVE ME ONE OF YOUR LONG, LOVING LECTURES ABOUT RESPONSIBILITIES AND "DOING THE RIGHT THING"!
NEXT MONTH: THE X-MEN

MARVEL® COMICS

X-MEN

JUN. '96 3

ONLY 99¢

APPROVED BY THE COMICS CODE AUTHORITY

THE ADVENTURES OF THE X-MEN®

DELIVERED INTO EVIL

GUEST-STARRING THE AMAZING SPIDER-MAN®!

Stan Lee Presents the Astonishing X-MEN
Child's Play
AN ORPHANAGE UNDER SIEGE ON NEW YORK CITY'S LOWER EAST SIDE--ATTACKED BY A VIOLENT GROUP CALLED THE FRIENDS OF HUMANITY...
...A GROWING ORGANIZATION WHOSE SOLE AIM IS TO SEPARATE FROM SOCIETY--BY FORCE, IF NECESSARY--THOSE BORN WITH SPECIAL ABILITIES...
...NAMELY MUTANTS!
MUTANTS ARE NOT HUMAN!
MUTANT SCUM!
GIVE US THAT STINKIN' MUTIE KID--OR WE'LL BURN THIS DUMP DOWN!
WE KNOW HE'S IN THERE! WE'RE TAKIN' HIM!
RALPH MACCHIO-WRITER
BEN HERRERA-PENCILER
MIKE MILLER-INKER
MICHAEL HIGGINS-LETTERER
MATT WEBB-COLORIST
MARK POWERS-EDITOR
BOB HARRAS-EDITOR IN CHIEF

GET HIM OUT HERE!

NO LOUSY MUTIE'S HIDIN' FROM US! WE'LL GET 'IM NO MATTER WHAT!

THREESH

FOLLOW ME! IF THEY WANT ADAM--THEY CAN HAVE HIM! HE'S A CREEP ANYWAY!
COME ON-- HE'S PROBABLY HIDIN' IN HIS ROOM UPSTAIRS!
AWRIGHT, WIMP! YOU'RE THE CAUSE OF ALL THIS! YOU'RE GOIN' OUT THERE!
NO! DON'T SEND ME OUT-- THEY'LL KILL ME!
I-I NEVER DID NOTHIN'! I'M JUST LIKE YOU GUYS! HONEST!
DON'T GIVE US THAT JUNK! IT'S 'CAUSE YOU AIN'T LIKE US THAT THEY WANT YOU!
NOW, YOU'RE COMIN'--ONE WAY OR THE OTHER!
HEY-- THE PUNK SLIPPED PAST US!
STAY AWAY! YOU'RE AS BAD AS THEY ARE! YOU'RE ALL THE SAME!

WHY CAN'T YOU JUST LEAVE ME ALONE?

JUST STAY BACK!
STAY BACK-- I'M WARNING YOU!
YOU'RE WARNING US?! WHATTAYA GONNA DO IF WE DON'T LISTEN, BLONDIE?

I MEAN IT!
I-I CAN'T HELP MYSELF-- CAN'T BE RESPONSIBLE FOR WHAT'S GONNA HAPPEN!
PLEASE-- GET LOST WHILE YOU'VE STILL GOT THE CHANCE!

HEY--LOOK AT 'IM! HIS EYES ARE ALL GLOWIN'!
YEAH--HE DON'T EVEN LOOK HUMAN NO MORE! MAN, THIS IS BAD!

STAY BAAAAACK!!

YAAAA--HE JUST MOVED HIS HANDS AND SOME KINDA FLAME WALL JUST SHOT UP IN FRONT OF US!
MAN, HE'S GOTTA BE A PYRO FREAK OR SOMETHIN'! LET'S BOOK!
I'M DITCHIN' IT!
THEY'RE ALL WAITING FOR ME DOWN THERE!
MUTANTS ARE SCUM!!
YOU DOWN THERE--
--YOU ALMOST MADE ME HURT MY FRIENDS!
YOU CREEPS REALLY WANT ME THAT BAD, HUH?
OKAY! IF THAT'S WHAT YOU WANT--HERE I COME! GET READY TO CATCH!
QUIT STALLIN' AND JUMP, MUTIE!
MARANATHA ORPHANAGE
MUTANTS MUST DIE!

AT THAT MOMENT, ENTER TWO X-MEN...
...STUDENTS OF PROFESSOR CHARLES XAVIER, THE WORLD'S MOST POWERFUL MUTANT MIND...
LOOKS LIKE OUR FRIEND DAT'S WORKIN' HERE AT DE ORPHANAGE ALERTED XAVIER 'BOUT DE MUTANT STAYIN' HERE JUST IN TIME.
SO IT WOULD SEEM, GAMBIT. I'LL BET DOLLARS TO DAFFODILS THESE CHARMERS ARE CHARTER MEMBERS OF THE INFAMOUS FRIENDS OF HUMANITY SECT WE'VE ENCOUNTERED SO OFTEN IN THE PAST.
GUESS DEY GOT WIND O' DE BOY STAYIN' HERE AN' FIGGERED ON DRAWIN' 'IM INTO DE OPEN.
AND THAT MUST BE THEIR QUARRY PERCHED PRECARIOUSLY ON YON LEDGE!
DE BOY GONNA JUMP, BEAST! WE GOTTA GET UP DERE AN' SAVE 'IM, N'EST-CE-PAS?
TIME THEN TO SHED THE CONFINING RAIMENT AS CIRCUMSTANCES DICTATE--
--AND EFFECT THE NIGH IMPOSSIBLE RESCUE IN MY INIMITABLE FASHION.
DRUM ROLL, PLEASE, MAESTRO!

GADZOOKS! THIS HAS THE SEEMING OF A JOYFUL SUNDAY IN THE STANDS AT VENERABLE GIANTS STADIUM! Ahh, THE MEMORIES!
NO! THE LAD WAS STRUCK BY A HURLED ROCK! HE'S BEEN DISLODGED FROM THE LEDGE!
IF HE ISN'T INTERCEPTED IN SCANT SECONDS--!
WHOK
HELP ME!
KILL THE MUTANTS!

THK
ROCK--KNOCKED ME OFF COURSE!
BUT THE BOY--!
CAN'T REACH HIM!
PLEASE--DON'T LET ME FALL!
Eh? A GAUDILY-COSTUMED FIGURE HAS SWUNG INTO THE FRAY TO SNAG THE LAD HASTILY!
I'VE GOT YOU, KID! JUST GO LIMP AND LEAVE IT ALL IN THE WEBBED HANDS OF--
--YOUR FRIENDLY, NEIGHBORHOOD SPIDER-MAN!
BETTER SET DOWN ON THE ROOF FAST--THIS KID'S TERRIFIED!

BACK OFF, PEOPLE! DE PARTY'S OVER! DESE KINETICALLY-CHARGED CARDS GONNA SEND YOU PACKIN', NON?
THSSSSSSS

HEY-- IT'S ANOTHER BLASTED MUTIE! AND HE'S THROWIN' SOME EXPLODING CARDS AT US!
L-LET'S GET HIM-- YI'KES!
THAASH

AND A LESS INSPIRING CALL TO ARMS I HAVE NE'ER HEARD ECHOED, MY GOOD MAN!
WHAT YOU NEED IS A REAL THREAT TO RALLY 'ROUND!

AND WHO BETTER THAN THE BLUSHING BEAST TO PROVIDE FOR YE?

Whoops! HOW CLUMSY OF MY PERIPATETIC PEDAL EXTREMITIES!
THOOMP

OKAAAAAY.

SWIFTLY, THE WONDROUS WEB-SPINNER--WHOSE NON-MUTANT POWERS DERIVE FROM THE BITE OF A RADIOACTIVE SPIDER--ENTERS THE FRAY...

...IN HIS OWN UNIQUE FASHION.

Tch! Tch! GENTLEMEN, **PLEASE**--IF YOU'RE CALLING YOURSELVES THE **FRIENDS** OF HUMANITY...

...THEN **LET'S** BE FRIENDS!

SHORTLY...
LET ME GET THIS STRAIGHT. YOU GUYS ARE MUTANTS, STUDENTS AT SOME ACADEMY IN WEST-CHESTER COUNTY--
--WHERE YOU TRY TO HELP OTHER MUTANTS ASSIMILATE INTO SOCIETY AND DEAL WITH THEIR POWERS.
ADAM HERE IS A MUTANT, TOO, AND YOU WERE OUT TO RESCUE HIM FROM THE FRIENDS OF HUMANITY WHEN I POPPED IN.
YOU GOT DAT RIGHT, HOMME.

WELL, THE FACT IS I ONLY HAVE YOUR WORD FOR THIS AND I'M NOT SURE I WANT TO JUST RELEASE THIS CHILD INTO YOUR CUSTODY.
YOU SAYIN' YOU DON' TRUST US?
WE'RE DE X-MEN--DE REAL T'ING!
GAMBIT, I'M SURE...
HEY, NO OFFENSE MEANT. LOOK, I HAVE AN IDEA THAT MAY PUT ALL OUR MINDS AT EASE-- EVEN ADAM'S.

THERE'S A BIOLOGIST I KNOW AT EMPIRE STATE UNIVERSITY*, CURT CONNORS, WHO MAY BE ABLE TO HELP ADAM. I'LL CONTACT HIM AND WE CAN ALL GO OVER THERE.
Hmmm... REASONABLE. AND THE CHANCE TO RUB ELBOWS WITH A FELLOW BIOCHEMIST OF CONNORS' REPUTE IS TEMPTING.
WHAT SAY YOU, CAJUN?
GOOD AS DONE.
STICK WIT' US, KID. EVERYT'ING GONNA BE JAKE.
*WHERE SPIDEY ATTENDS AS A GRADUATE STUDENT IN HIS CIVILIAN IDENTITY AS PETER PARKER. --Professor Powers

SO, THEY'RE OFF TO CONNORS' LAB. IT'S TIME I CALLED AHEAD TO LET HIM KNOW OF MY OWN ARRIVAL.
WOW! WILL YOU SHOW ME SOME COOL CARD TRICKS, MR. GAMBIT?
YOU GONNA BE A RIVERBOAT GAMBLER 'FORE I'M T'ROUGH, BOY!

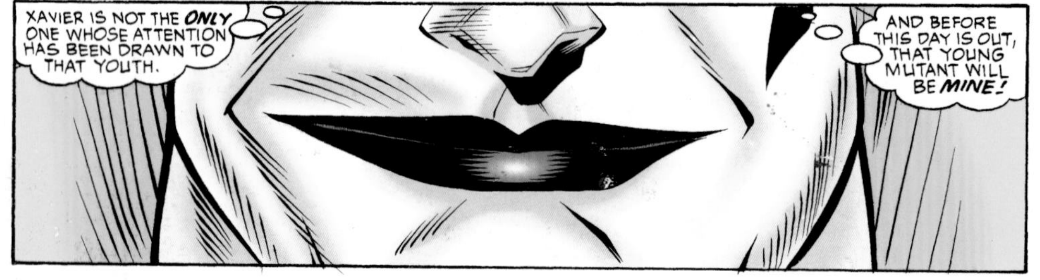
XAVIER IS NOT THE ONLY ONE WHOSE ATTENTION HAS BEEN DRAWN TO THAT YOUTH.
AND BEFORE THIS DAY IS OUT, THAT YOUNG MUTANT WILL BE MINE!

ONE OF THE MANY SCIENCE BUILDINGS AT EMPIRE STATE UNIVERSITY IN THE HEART OF MANHATTAN...
...WHERE BIOLOGIST CURT CONNORS OCCUPIES A SUITE OF LABS.
Ahhh, THAT MUST BE THEM.
NOK NOK
Uh, WELCOME. WHEN YOU SAID YOU WERE BEING ACCOMPANIED BY SOME FRIENDS, I NEVER IMAGINED...
QUITE A GROUP, I KNOW.
DR. CONNORS, GOOD TO SEE YOU AGAIN. THIS IS THE BOY ADAM I TOLD YOU ABOUT ON THE PHONE.
AND THESE GENTLEMEN ARE HIS "GUARDIANS"--MEMBERS OF THE MUTANT GROUP, THE X-MEN. THIS IS REMY LeBEAU, FROM THE BIG EASY...
...AND THIS IS DR. HENRY McCOY, THE NOTED BIOCHEMIST.
GOOD TO SEE YOU AGAIN,* SPIDER-MAN. I'M ANXIOUS TO HELP THIS LAD.
AND, OF COURSE, I'VE HEARD OF DR. McCOY. MY FACILITIES ARE AT YOUR DISPOSALS.
A VERITABLE RESEARCH WONDERLAND, SIR. THANK YOU.
MAN, LOOK AT ALL THIS NEAT STUFF!
* SPIDEY HAS AIDED THE GOOD DOCTOR ON MANY AN OCCASION. --Good Powers.
ADAM, I FIRST WANT TO PERFORM SOME ROUTINE TESTS.
WE'LL TAKE SOME BLOOD AND LOOK AT IT UNDER THE MICRO-SCOPE.
PLATELET COUNT--IN ORDER... PROTEINS--GLOBULIN AND ALBUMIN, STABLE. SALTS, SUGAR, URIC ACID AND CREATININ--ALL IN PROPER TRACE AMOUNTS. LEUCOCYTES--FINE.
THEY'RE ALL WITHIN NORMAL PARAMETERS, DOCTOR CONNORS.
GOOD. THEN WE'LL PROCEED WITH A MORE DETAILED EXAMINATION.

A BATTERY OF TESTS IS PERFORMED, MEASURING HEARTRATE, RESPIRATION AND BODY TEMPERATURE.

YOU'RE HEALTHY AS A HORSE, SON. NOW I WANT TO TEST THE EXTENT OF YOUR SPECIAL *ABILITIES*.

"FIRST, I WANT YOU TO TRY TO IGNITE THAT PIECE OF PAPER--

"--THEN, THE SAME TO THIS PIECE OF WOOD...

"...AND FINALLY, TRY TO MELT THIS METAL BAR."

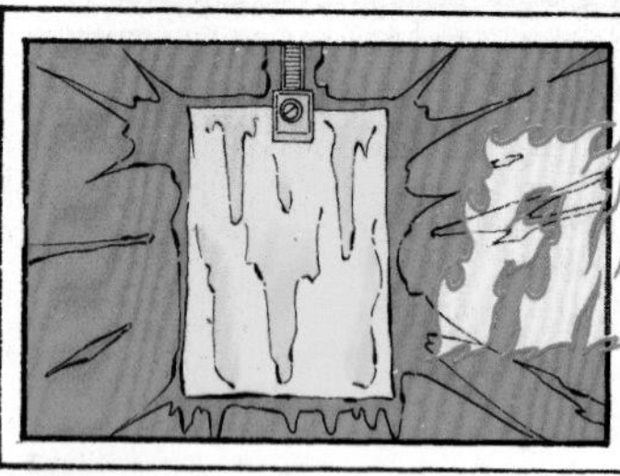

LAD, THE VERY NEXT WEENIE ROAST HOSTED BY YOURS TRULY WILL HAVE YOU AS THE **GUEST OF HONOR**.

YOU **MEAN** IT?

GOTTA BE LEAVIN' NOW, DR. CONNORS. DERE'S SOME... "PAPERWORK" DAT'S GOTTA BE DONE BACK AT DE ORPHANAGE.

BE BACK SOON, *MES AMIS*.

GOOD MEETING YOU, MR. LE BEAU. I'VE GOTTA SPLIT, TOO.

DON'T LET HIM BURN THE PLACE DOWN, OKAY, DOC?

YES. YOU HAVE MY WORD ON IT, SPIDER-MAN. THERE IS STILL MUCH MORE TO DO. TAKE CARE.

DAT BOY'S GOT POWER DAT SOMEDAY WILL **RIVAL** ANY O' DE X-MEN'S. JUST HOPE HE AIN'T GONNA GO T'ROUGH DE **SUFFERIN'** WE DID.

MAN, SPIDER POWERS ARE **ONE** THING, BUT THE ABILITY TO SET THINGS ON FIRE...

...THAT'S THE KIND OF GREAT POWER THAT **REALLY** CREATES SOME HEAVY RESPONSIBILITY!

T'ANKS FOR ALERTIN' US TO ADAM'S PRESENCE HERE AT DE ORPHANAGE, PHILIP.
NO PROBLEM, GAMBIT. AS A MEMBER OF CHARLES XAVIER'S UNDERGROUND, IT'S MY DUTY TO KEEP TABS ON ANYONE WE SUSPECT MAY BE A MUTANT...
...FOR THEIR **OWN** SAFETY.

YEAH, LIKE CEREBRO* AIN'T ENOUGH FOR PICKIN' UP TRACES O' NEW MUTANT TYPES.
I HEAR XAVIER'S GOT PEOPLE LIKE ME **EVERYWHERE**--EVEN THE GOVERNMENT.
*THE MUTANT-DETECTING DEVICE AT THE X-MANSION. --Mr. Mark.

HE DON'T LEAVE **NO** STONE UNTURNED, **DAT'S** FOR SURE. Y'KNOW, SOMETIMES DAT MAN'S A LITTLE SPOOKY, PHILIP.

GOOD DAY, DR. CONNORS. MOST KIND OF YOU TO INVITE ME HERE TO SEE THIS REMARKABLE YOUNG MAN.

AND WHO IS THIS OTHER GENTLEMAN?

HE'S DOCTOR HENRY McCOY, A WELL-KNOWN BIOCHEMIST HERE IN THE STATES.

YES, OF COURSE. MOST *PLEASED* TO MEET YOU.

LIKEWISE...

Hmmm, METHINKS SOMETHING IS DISTINCTLY *FAMILIAR* ABOUT THE GOOD DOCTOR ESSEX.

BUT WHAT 'TIS, I CANNOT PLACE MY FURRY FINGER UPON AT THE MOMENT.

DR. ESSEX, THESE ARE THE RATHER ASTONISHING RESULTS OF ADAM'S PYROKINETIC PROWESS.
WE WERE JUST ABOUT TO TEST THE LAD'S ABILITIES ON A LEAD BAR. AS YOU KNOW, SIR, LEAD HAS A HIGHER MELTING POINT THAN MOST METALS. SO...
YES, YES. SHALL WE GET ON WITH IT THEN?

ADAM, CONCENTRATE ON THE CYLINDER IN FRONT OF YOU. DO AS YOU DID BEFORE.
TRY TO MELT IT, BUT DO SO **CAREFULLY**... CONTROL YOUR ABILITY.

SHRRRKKLLL

OKAY, THAT'S ALL, SON. YOU DIDN'T MELT IT, BUT YOU GOT THE LEAD RED HOT.
WE DON'T WANT YOU STRAINING YOURSELF...

I DO NOT BELIEVE THIS BOY HAS COME ANYWHERE NEAR EXHIBITING HIS FULL POTENTIAL. I SAY CONTINUE.
DR. ESSEX, NO DISRESPECT, SIR, BUT YOU AREN'T IN CHARGE HERE.
OH, INDEED I AM.
WHAT'S GOING ON HERE? I-- OOOFF!
BE QUIET, YOU FOOL!
THAT SHOULD HOLD YOU FOR THE NONCE!
SOME TYPE OF STASIS FIELD. I'M UNABLE TO MOVE--CAN'T EVEN SPEAK!
ZZMM
NOW, BOY! YOU KNOW YOU CAN DO BETTER! THEY'RE JUST LIKE ALL THE OTHERS!
THEY DON'T WANT YOU TO REALLY TAP INTO YOUR POWER! THEY WANT YOU TO FEEL WEAK--UNDER THEIR THUMB.
BUT I KNOW WHAT'S BEST FOR YOU, ADAM! I AM YOUR ONLY FRIEND!
NOW MELT THE LEAD. MELT IT!
SPLUSSH
MARVELOUS! CHILD! FEEL THE POWER SURGING THROUGH YOU!
FWOOH
NO! DON'T GO ANY FURTHER! THINGS BEHIND THE LEAD ARE CATCHING FIRE! STOP IT!

ESSEX IS CHANGING-- UNDERGOING SOME PHYSICAL TRANSFORMATION! NOW I KNOW WHY HIS BEARDED COUNTENANCE SMACKED OF THE FAMILIAR!
IN REALITY, THE SUAVE, SOPHISTICATED SIRRAH IS--
--SINISTER!
NO NEED TO FEAR ME, ADAM. I AM MUCH THE SAME AS YOU. A WORLD OF INFERIOR HUMANS HATES US BECAUSE WE ARE DIFFERENT... BETTER THAN THEY ARE.
BUT YOU WILL LEARN FROM ME, BOY. YOU WILL DISCOVER HOW BEST TO USE YOUR ABILITIES AND TURN THE TABLES ON ANY WHO WOULD OPPOSE YOU!
I SEE A GREAT FUTURE FOR YOU, ADAM. A GLORIOUS FUTURE AT MY SIDE!
HE'S LOST CONTROL OF THE STASIS FIELD MOMENTARILY! TIME TO TAKE ADVANTAGE OF THE SITUATION--
--AND HAVE HIRSUTE HENRY McCOY STOP THE SCINTILLATING SHENANIGANS!
Ahhh, MR. SINISTER, MY GOOD MAN.
WOULDST THOU BE SO KIND AS TO SWIVEL YOUR SHINY, SIMONIZED SELF AROUND TOWARD MINE APPROACHING APPENDAGES?
THE SUPER HEROES HANDBOOK EXPRESSLY FORBIDS RENDING ADVERSARIES ASSUNDER FROM BEHIND!
THE BEAST. A LOQUACIOUS BORE... AS ALWAYS.

PROBLEMS LIKE DIS ARE WHAT DE X-MEN'S ALL ABOUT. DAT'S WHY WE GOTTA GET DE CHILD UP TO XAVIER AND IN OUR CUSTODY.
I'M NOT SURE I LIKE THE SOUND OF THAT.
WAITAMINNIT... I LEFT ADAM WITH DR. CONNORS AND-- McCOY-- THE BEAST!
THERE'S SOMETHING FISHY ABOUT THIS BUNCH OF RENEGADE MUTANTS.
WHICH IS WHY I'D BETTER GET BACK TO EMPIRE STATE U, FAST BEFORE THE BOY GETS KIDNAPPED OR SOMETHING.
HERE IT IS. AND THAT'S CONNORS' WINDOW JUST BELOW.

* THE SIXTH SENSE SPIDER-MAN POSSESSES THAT WARNS HIM OF DANGER.
-- No-Sense Powers.

HEY, CURLY! YOU WANNA COME ALONG PEACEFULLY, OR IS THIS GOING TO GET MESSY?
ADAM! THAT IS ANOTHER BAD MAN WHO WANTS TO TAKE YOU AWAY AND HURT YOU!
YES--HE'S A VERY, VERY BAD MAN! STOP HIM NOW!
I DON'T LIKE YOU, MISTER.
Eh? ANOTHER ANNOYANCE?
SHEESH! THE KID JUST LOOKED NASTY AT ME AND THE WALL EXPLODED IN FLAMES!
IF HE GROWS UP TO BE A SUPER-VILLAIN-- I'M RETIRING EARLY.
BAWHOOM
Oops! MY TRUSTY SPIDER-SENSE S WARNING ME THAT TALL 'N' GRUESOME'S RUSHING ME!
STAND STILL! WHAT MANNER OF CREATURE ARE YOU?
THEPP
WHAT MANNER OF CREATURE AM I? WELL, AT LEAST I DON'T LOOK LIKE I WASHED MY FACE WITH TOOTHPASTE THIS MORNING, BUNKIE!
OWWW! I ALMOST BROKE MY HAND ON THAT METALLIC HIDE OF HIS!
WHUNKK!

OH, BOY! CONNORS AND McCOY ARE REAL **CLOSE** TO THE FLAMES!
THEIR ONLY CHANCE IS IF MY SPECIAL ***LIQUID WEBBING*** CAN DOUSE THE FIRE!
HAVE TO DO IT FAST OR I'M A ***SITTING DUCK*** FOR THIS GUY!
SPLUSH

INTERESTING... THAT MACHINERY ABOVE HIM.

GREAT! IT'S WORKING.

ADAM, YOU CAN STOP THE BAD MAN.

JUST MELT THE CABLES ON THAT MACHINE OVER HIS HEAD. LISTEN TO ME BOY! DO IT!

THIS WILL STOP THE BAD MAN.

TAWHAM

SPIDER-SENSE ***WARNING*** ME--CAN'T GET OUT OF THE WAY ***IN TIME!***

SO, YOU ARE STILL CONSCIOUS, INSECT. ALLOW ME TO EASE YOUR BURDEN.
Uhhh...

YOU WILL NOT FEEL THE WEIGHT AFTER THIS.
THAMP

YOU DID WELL, YOUNG ADAM. WE STOPPED THE BAD MEN WHO WANTED TO HURT YOU.
YOU SEE HOW WELL WE WORKED TOGETHER. DID YOU LIKE IT?
OKAY... BUT DID WE HAVE TO HURT THEM SO BAD? I-- I DON'T LIKE HURTING PEOPLE.

OH, AND NEITHER DO I. BUT I ONLY DID WHAT HAD TO BE DONE SO THEY WOULDN'T HURT YOU! DO YOU SEE NOW?
I GUESS SO.

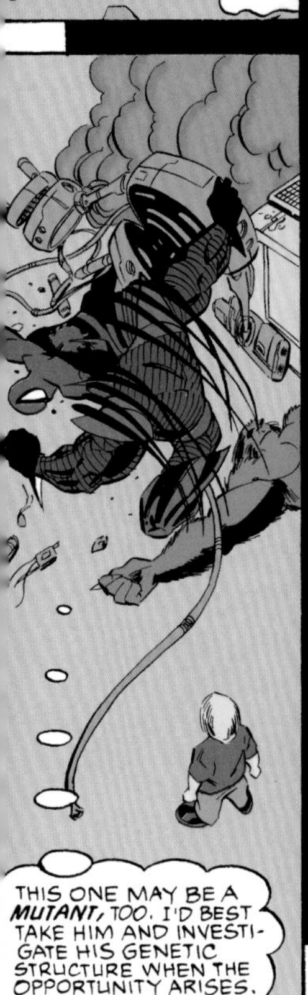
THIS ONE MAY BE A MUTANT, TOO. I'D BEST TAKE HIM AND INVESTIGATE HIS GENETIC STRUCTURE WHEN THE OPPORTUNITY ARISES.

WE MUST LEAVE NOW. SOME BAD MEN WILL COME HERE SHORTLY AND TAKE THESE TWO AWAY. WE MUST NOT BE HERE WHEN THEY COME.
WHY ARE YOU CARRYING THIS GUY?

OH... I HAVE HEARD THAT HE IS NOT AS EVIL AS THE OTHER TWO.
THERE IS A CHANCE THAT WE MAY TURN HIM TO OUR SIDE, MAKE HIM GOOD AS WE ARE.
WOULDN'T YOU LIKE TO HAVE ANOTHER FRIEND, ADAM? WOULD THAT MAKE YOU HAPPY?
Y'KNOW, I DON'T HAVE ANY REAL FRIENDS. IT MIGHT BE FUN, MISTER.

INDEED. ONE MIGHT EVEN DESCRIBE IT AS--CHILD'S PLAY.
SLAMM
TO BE CONTINUED IN THE PAGES OF THE ADVENTURES OF SPIDER-MAN!

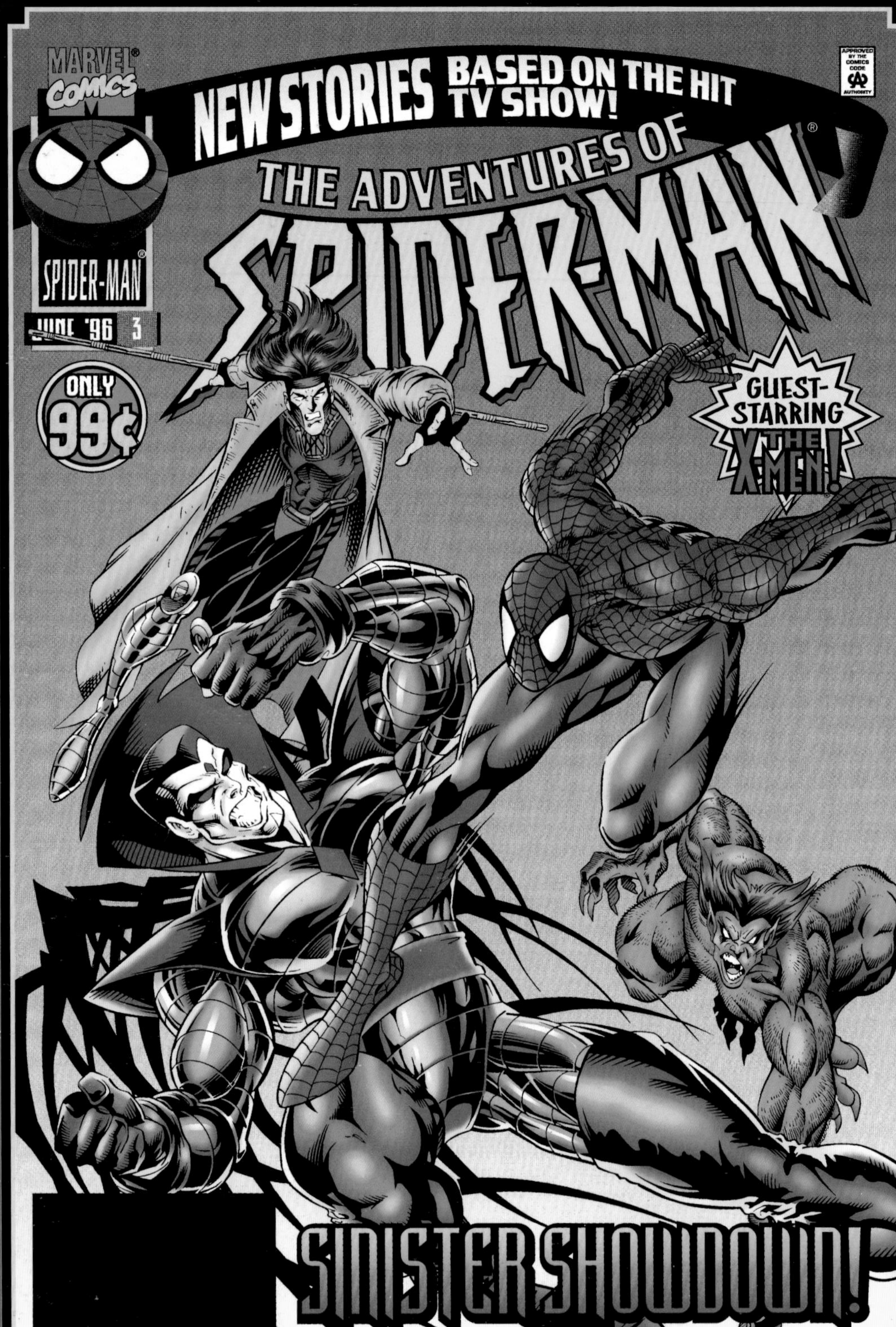
MARVEL COMICS
NEW STORIES BASED ON THE HIT TV SHOW!
THE ADVENTURES OF SPIDER-MAN
SPIDER-MAN
JUNE '96 3
ONLY 99¢
GUEST-STARRING THE X-MEN!
APPROVED BY THE COMICS CODE AUTHORITY
SINISTER SHOWDOWN!

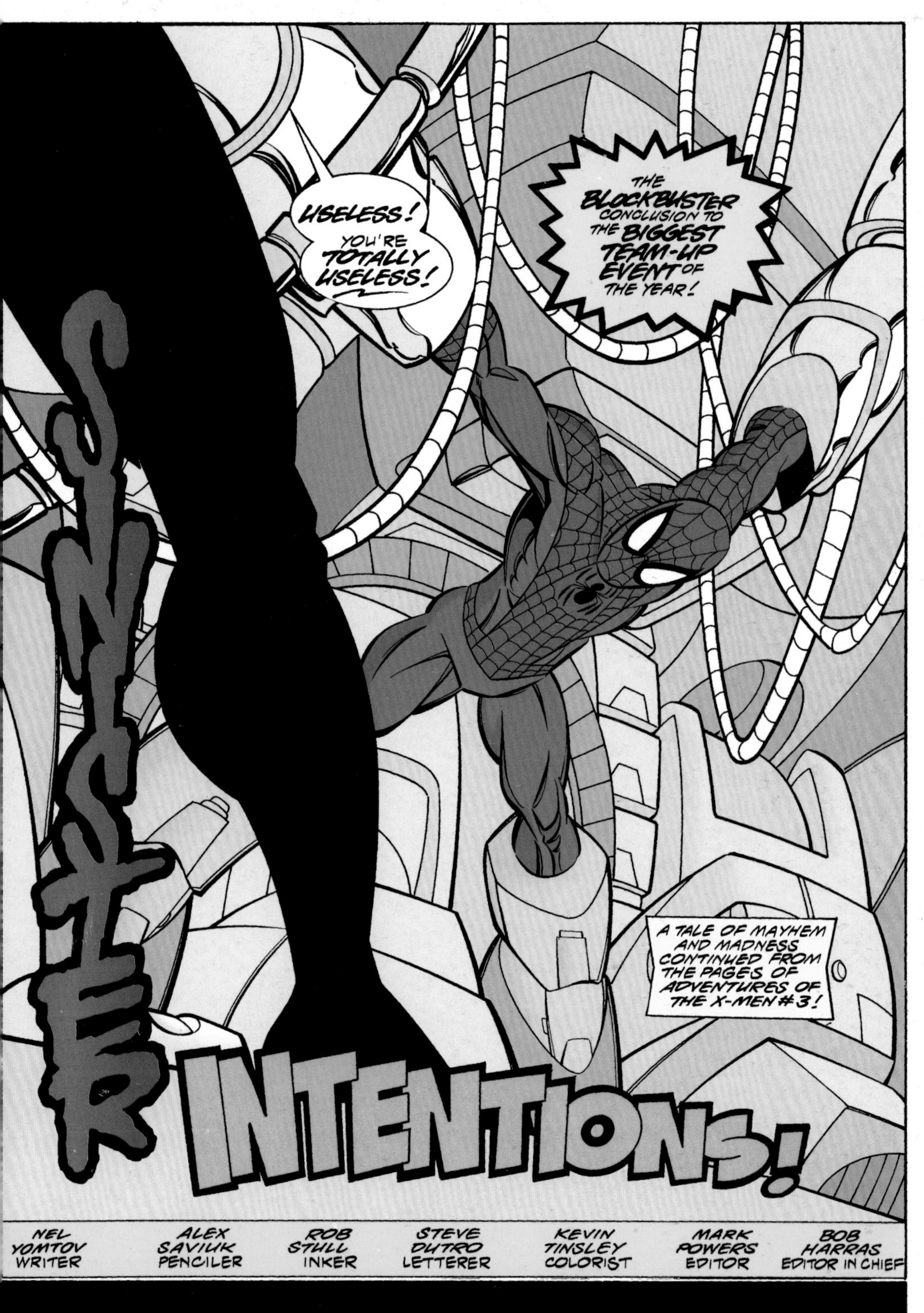
USELESS! YOU'RE TOTALLY USELESS!
THE BLOCKBUSTER CONCLUSION TO THE BIGGEST TEAM-UP EVENT OF THE YEAR!
A TALE OF MAYHEM AND MADNESS CONTINUED FROM THE PAGES OF ADVENTURES OF THE X-MEN #3!
SINISTER INTENTIONS!
NEL YOMTOV WRITER
ALEX SAVIUK PENCILER
ROB STULL INKER
STEVE DUTRO LETTERER
KEVIN TINSLEY COLORIST
MARK POWERS EDITOR
BOB HARRAS EDITOR IN CHIEF

I SHOULD HAVE LEFT YOU TO BURN WITH CONNORS AND THE BEAST IN THE LABORATORY FIRE!
ALL THESE WASTED HOURS OF PAINSTAKING EXAMINATION REVEAL WHAT I THOUGHT ALL ALONG...
YOU ARE NOT A MUTANT!
ALL YOU HAD TO DO WAS ASK, FROSTY! YOU THINK I ENJOY BEING PRODDED AND POKED LIKE A GUINEA PIG?
ENOUGH OF THE MAD SCIENTIST BIT, MR. SINISTER. NOW YOU LISTEN UP...
...I'M INTERESTED IN ONLY ONE THING...
...AND THAT'S THE WELFARE OF THAT POOR KID ADAM.
I'M INTERESTED IN HIM, TOO, SPIDER-MAN... ALTHOUGH FOR QUITE DIFFERENT REASONS.
COME HERE, LAD...
S-SURE, MR. SINISTER...
...LET ME TELL YOU MORE ABOUT THIS BAD MAN.

HE IS THE ONE RESPONSIBLE FOR TAKING YOU TO PROFESSOR CONNORS' LAB WHERE THE X-MEN ENGAGED YOU IN THOSE FRIGHTENING EXPERIMENTS.
WHEN I ARRIVED TO RESCUE YOU, WASN'T IT SPIDER-MAN WHO TRIED TO PREVENT ME?
YOU KNOW HOW MUCH HE SCARES YOU! THAT IS WHY YOU USED YOUR POWERS TO HELP ME SUBDUE HIM IN THE LAB!
DON'T BELIEVE THAT GARBAGE, ADAM!
I DON'T KNOW WHY, BUT HE'S THE ONE WHO'S GONNA HURT YOU!
NONSENSE! WE'RE FRIENDS, ADAM. IT IS HE WHO WISHES TO HARM YOU.
PEOPLE LIKE HIM FEAR AND HATE US... SIMPLY BECAUSE OF OUR UNIQUE AND ENVIABLE ABILITIES.
FREE YOURSELF FROM THE TERROR HE CAUSES YOU, ADAM.
USE YOUR POWERS...
MNGHH!
MNGHH!
FSSSSS
MNGHH!
YEAAH!
F-ZAACK
O-OKAY... IF YOU THINK IT'S ALL RIGHT, MR. SINISTER...
NOT AGAIN! ADAM!
NOOOO!

AT EXACTLY THAT MOMENT...

GOOD T'ING DE ADMINISTRATOR IS SENSITIVE TO ADAM'S SPECIAL NEEDS. OTHER-WISE --

-- HE WOULD NOT HAVE ALLOWED SPIDER-MAN, HANK AND ME TO TAKE HIM TO DE SAFETY OF EMPIRE STATE UNIVERSITY.

I CANNOT HELP BUT FEEL SORRY FOR DE BOY...

WHO'S THAT?

I WONDER WHAT HE WAS DOING AT THE ORPHANAGE!

NON.

MON DIEU.

THE SCIENCE BUILDING!
I PRAY DAT MY FRIENDS ARE NOT TRAPPED INSIDE!
HANK! DERE IS TOO MUCH SMOKE FOR ME TO SEE!
WHERE ARE YOU, MON AMI?!
ANSWER ME!
REMY... BACK HERE... BEHIND YOU...
HANK!
EASY. WE'LL BE OUT OF HERE SOON, HOMME.
WHERE IS DE PROFESSEUR CONNORS... AND ADAM?
THEY WERE HERE IN THE LAB WITH ME...
BUT NNORS' IEND WAS ISTER IN SGUISE!
I-I DON'T KNOW WHAT HAPPENED TO THEM AFTER THAT.
LET ME GET YOU IN DE HALL FOR SOME FRESH AIR-- THEN I'LL GO BACK INSIDE!

SECONDS LATER...
PROFESSEUR CONNORS! C'EST MOI... GAMBIT! ARE YOU IN HERE?
PROFESSEUR?!
KAFF SMOKE... HEAT... IT'S UNBEARABLE...
CAN'T KAFF KAFF BREATHE...
PLEASE... HELP...
LET'S GET GOIN' 'FOR DE FIRE STARTS TO--
BRACK
FOOSH
--BRING DE WHOLE FLAMIN' PLACE DOWN ON US!
KROOOM
YAAIII!
YOU'LL BE FINE, BUT TELL ME-- WHERE IS DE BOY?
WHAT HAS HAPPENED TO ADAM?
HE'S NOT HERE. HE MUST'VE BEEN TAKEN BY THE MADMAN WHO KNOCKED ME OUT.
PLEASE... I NEED FRESH AIR...

SHORTLY...
YOUR "ASSOCIATE" IS MUCH MORE THAN YOU THOUGHT HIM TO BE--
--A TWISTED GENIUS OBSESSED WITH CONTROLLING MUTANT GENEALOGY--
--AND ONE OF OUR GREATEST ENEMIES-- SINISTER!
I FOUND IT WHEN I WAS GROPING AROUND IN THE FIRE. IT'S SPIDER-MAN'S.
I'VE KNOWN HIM A FEW WEEKS-- WE MET AT A CONFERENCE ON BIOGENETICS. HE SEEMED INTERESTED IN MY RESEARCH.
MY GUESS IS THAT HE WAS HERE AFTER BEAST AND I GOT KNOCKED OUT AND DROPPED IT IN A SCUFFLE WITH THAT MADMAN.
BLAST! I DIDN'T TRUST THAT GUY FROM THE MINUTE HE WALKED INTO THE LAB. NOW HE HAS ADAM!
SAY, PROFESSOR... WHAT'S THAT IN YOUR HAND?
IT'S A TRANSMITTER HE USES FOR TRACKING PURPOSES.
SPIDER-MAN MUST HAVE THE RECEIVING COMPONENT WITH HIM. MAYBE IF I TINKER WITH THIS--
SAY NO MORE, DOCTOR. I'LL SET YOU UP WITH ALL THE SUPPLIES YOU NEED.
YOU T'INK THAT WHEN WE BE FINDIN' SPIDER-MAN...
...WE MAYBE FIND ADAM AND THE MYSTERY MAN, TOO, NON?
PRECISELY. I JUST HOPE SPIDER-MAN IS HAVING AN EASIER TIME WITH SINISTER THAN I DID...!

ADAM'S MUTANT PYROKINETIC POWER IS AS INTENSE AS ANY I'VE SEEN... HE'S SLICED THROUGH THESE MANACLES LIKE THEY WERE BUTTER!
IF I DON'T STOP HIM SOON, I'M GONNA END UP BEING TONIGHT'S EXTRA CRISPY BARBEQUE APPETIZER!
HIS LIES HAVE DELAYED US LONG ENOUGH!
IT'S TIME WE CONTINUED TO GET TO KNOW EACH OTHER.
SNAP OUT OF IT, ADAM! SINISTER'S GOT YOU UNDER SOME KIND OF SPELL! HE'S MAKIN' YOU HURT ME!
FIGHT OFF HIS CONTROL! I KNOW YOU CAN DO IT!
OKAY...
GOOD BOY. YOU CAN EVEN MEET THE FRIENDS I'VE TOLD YOU ABOUT.
I KNOW YOU'LL ENJOY THEIR COMPANY... THEY'RE SO MUCH LIKE YOU.
NOW, ADAM... DESTROY SPIDER-MAN!
SHRIPP
WHAT--?! YOU?!

SHRIPPP
MAYBE YOU BEEN EXPECTIN' CHEF PRUDHOMME WIT' A BOWL OF SHRIMP GUMBO, OUI?
SINISTER! I SHOULD'VE KNOWN THAT YOU WERE WHAT THE SICK FEELING IN MY STOMACH AT ESU WAS TRYING TO TELL ME!
THIS WHOLE CAPER OF SCIENTIFIC EXPERIMENTATION WITH MUTANTS HAS GOT YOUR SMELL ALL OVER IT!
WELL, I'VE GOT NEWS FOR YOU-- IT'S TIME WE GET RID OF THE STENCH!
KRANG
CLEVER, DOCTOR, BUT ADAM IS THE ISSUE...
...AND HE'S NOT GOING ANYWHERE!
NICE TIMING, X-MEN! MAYBE NOW I CAN FINALLY GET THROUGH TO ADAM!
ADAM! LISTEN UP, SON!
WHOAA!
IT'S NO USE! HE'S TOTALLY ZONKED OUT BY EVERYTHING THAT'S HAPPENED TO HIM!
HOW MUCH MORE CAN THIS POOR KID TAKE?
THE TIME HAS COME TO MEET YOUR NEW FRIENDS, ADAM...
SAY HELLO--

"--TO THE NASTY BOYS!"
SLAB DOESN'T LIKE UNINVITED GUESTS, X-MEN!
DOESN'T LIKE THEM AT ALL!
A NOBLE THOUGHT, MY FRIEND, BUT WHERE'S YOUR SENSE OF COURTESY AND CIVILITY?
RUCKUS, WHILE YOU TWO JIVE... HAIRBAG AND ME WILL BURY THEM ALIVE!
YA GOT THAT, GORGEOUS GEORGE? I BEEN WAITIN' FOR A REMATCH WITH THE BLUE FURRY ONE FOR A LONG TIME!
DESTROY THEM!
HOPE WE NOT BE INTERRUPTIN' DEM FROM SOMET'IN' IMPORTANT!
HARDLY WHAT COULD THEY BE DOING SITTING ON THEIR DUFFS IN A BACK ROOM?
PARDONEZ-MOI, MON AMI, BUT P'HAPS DEY WAS PLAYIN' A FRIENDLY--

--GAME O'CARDS!
I CUT DEM--USE MY MUTANT POWER TO KINETICALLY CHARGE DEM UP--AND--
--VOILA!
KKRKLL
YOU COME UP EMPTY-HANDED, CAJUN MAN!
NOW IT'S THE NASTY BOYS' TURN TO DEAL
KROOM
KROOM
THOSE TWO BETTER LEAVE US MORE THAN JUST SCRAPS, GEORGE!
HSS
DON'T COUNT ON IT! HAIRBAG'S LETHAL BREATH IS ENOUGH TO KILL BOTH OF 'EM!
ADAM WAS IN BAD SHAPE! WE'VE GOT TO GET HIM AWAY FROM SINISTER!
EASIER SAID THAN DONE, MON AMI! RIGHT NOW, IT APPEARS SPIDER-MAN IS DE BOY'S ONLY HOPE!

SINISTER'S JOININ' THE BRAWL! THAT LEAVES ME ALONE WITH ADAM...
...AND WITH HIM NOT PAYING ATTENTION TO ME, THIS IS THE LAST CHANCE I GET TO BUST OUTTA THESE THINGS...
HOPE HE'S WEAKENED THESE MANACLES ENOUGH TO DO IT...
URNN
GOTTA BREAK FREE...
...IF I CAN'T...
URNN
...ADAM WILL BE LEFT TO SINISTER'S TENDER MERCIES...
...HE'LL NEVER HAVE A SHOT AT A NORMAL, HAPPY LIFE!
SHRAK
YES!
LET'S SEE YOUR PAL MR. SINISTER DO THAT, KID!
SHRAK
SHRAK
SHRAK
WHOAA... NEAT.
I'LL SAY! I'M PRETTY IMPRESSED MYSELF!
YOU STAY HERE! DON'T MOVE!
NOW TO JOIN THE PARTY ALREADY IN PROGRESS!

METHINKS YOU NASTY BOYS HAVE A SHORT MEMORY, SLAB.
THE LAST TIME WE MET, THE X-MEN MOPPED UP A SOUTH PACIFIC JUNGLE WITH YOUR HIDES!
KRONK
HERE'S HOW WE DID IT--!
YOU'RE LIVIN' IN THE PAST, YA PUNY RUNT...
FWAKK!
HERE AND NOW IS THE ONLY THING THAT COUNTS!
UNFF!
DAT SPITEFUL REMARK ABOUT MON AMI'S FURRY CONDITION SURPRISED ME...
...OR AIN'T YOU LOOKED AT YOURSELF IN A MIRROR LATELY?
JAB
KIND O' LIKE DE KETTLE CALLING DE POT BLACK, NON?
YOU FOREIGNERS GOT A WAY WITH WORDS, CAJUN...
...BUT HOW GOOD ARE YA GONNA BE HANDLING THESE PEARLY WHITES OF MINE?
cough kakk cough
IT AIN'T FAIR YOU LETTIN' SLAB AND HAIRBAG HAVE ALL THE FUN, MR. SINISTER!
SOMETIMES I THINK YOU PLAY FAVORITES AROUND HERE!
HUH?! HOW DID--

HI HO, NASTY BOYS!
Y'KNOW, WITH A NAME LIKE THAT, YOU GUYS OUGHTA GIVE SOME THOUGHT TO BECOMING A RAP GROUP...
...'CAUSE AS SUPER-VILLAINS, YOU'RE A BUNCH OF TOTAL LOSERS!
SINISTER!
YES, NASTIES. NOW DESTROY HIM.
KRAK
WUNGH!
AWFF!
KRAK
HERE'S A MESSAGE FOR YOU, SPIDER-MAN...
YAAHHH
HE'S YOURS, GEORGE! FINISH HIM!
YOU MUST BE READIN' MY MIND, RUCKUS!
CHOKE ON THIS, BUG-EYES!
HE'S STRETCHING LIKE RUBBER!

YOU COMPLAINED THAT I HELD YOU BACK FROM CONTRIBUTING TO THE BATTLE, GORGEOUS GEORGE...
NOW SHOW ME THAT I WAS WRONG... KILL HIM!
SNUFF HIM OUT, GEORGE! SNUFF HIM ALL THE WAY OUT!
HMM. COZY.
I CAN'T FIGURE THESE GUYS...
...WITH SUCH COOL MUTANT POWERS...
...YOU'D THINK THEY'D COME UP WITH SOMETHING BETTER THAN...
YAIII!
...A FIFTH-RATE REED RICHARDS!*
HOLY HANNAH!
SHRAKK
YOU'VE DONE WELL AGAINST MY UNDER-LINGS--
--BUT NOW YOU MUST DEAL WITH MR. SINISTER--
--AND AS YOU SHALL SOON SEE--
--HE IS THE REAL THING!
*MR. FANTASTIC OF THE FANTASTIC 4! --MARK

STAND ASIDE, NASTY BOYS, AND WITNESS WHY IT IS THAT I'M CALLED SINISTER!
I'M GOING TO GIVE YOU ALL QUITE A SHOW...
HEY, NO FAIR! I'M GETTIN' ACED OUT OF ANOTHER SHOT AT THEM!
DAT'S SHAMEFUL! YOU EVER HEAR SUCH WORDS OF DISRESPECT IN ALL O' YOUR LIFE, SPIDER-MAN?
NEVER! IT'S EITHER REAL HARD TO FIND GOOD HELP THESE DAYS OR THE GENE POOL IN THIS CROWD, IS AWFULLY SHALLOW!
WHOA! I'D WATCH WHAT I WAS SAYING ABOUT GENE POOLS IN THIS CROWD, SPIDER-MAN!
WE MUTANTS ARE KIND OF SENSITIVE TO CRACKS LIKE THAT!
BESIDES, ISN'T THIS THE CUSTOMARY JUNCTURE AT WHICH ONE OF THE HEROES VOCIFERATES--
CHARGE!
THWIP
OL' REMY LIKES DE SOUN' OF DAT, MON AMI!
THWIP
Y-YEAH, ME TOO, BIG BLUE!
"VOCIFERATES"? SHEESH!
SHTOOOM
ENOUGH!

I TIRE OF THIS! BACK OFF, NASTY BOYS...
...I ALREADY HAVE WHAT I SOUGHT IN THE FIRST PLACE!
IT WAS IMPERATIVE FOR ME TO STUDY THIS BOY WHO SO EARLY IN LIFE HAD MANIFESTED SUCH DAZZLING MUTANT ABILITIES.
THE TESTS YOU SAW ME PERFORM AT ESU CONFIRMED MY INITIAL BELIEFS...
...BUT IT IS THE DNA SAMPLES I EXTRACTED FROM HIM THAT WILL PROVIDE ME WITH THE GENETIC MATERIAL TO CREATE GENERATIONS OF UNSTOPPABLE MUTANTS--ALL UNDER MY ABSOLUTE CONTROL!
THWIP
WHAT THE HECK IS HE TALKIN' ABOUT, BEAST?
THWIP
BEATS ME. I'M AS PUZZLED AS YOU.
NOW IF YOU'LL EXCUSE US, WE HAVE MORE PRESSING MATTERS TO ATTEND...
SHOULDN'T WE TAKE THE KID IN CASE YOU NEED HIM AGAIN, MR. SINISTER?
NOW, WE CAN COME BACK FOR HIM ANYTIME. I WANT TO BEGIN WORK ON THESE SAMPLES IMMEDIATELY!
HAH! HIS OWN WEBBING IS STOPPIN' THEM FROM COMIN' AFTER US!
COME ON! BEFORE THEY GET TOO FAR!
--ADAM?
NO! LET 'EM GO! WE GOTTA GO BACK AND CHECK ON--
BADOOM!

GAMBIT... HELP ME... IT HURTS SO MUCH...
FZZZZZZZAK
HOLY--! HE'S BURNIN' LIKE A SUPER-NOVA!
OH, MY STARS AND GARTERS...
AIN'T SEEN NOTHIN' LIKE DIS SINCE JEAN GREY'S PHOENIX PROBLEMS!
SKIP THE HISTORY LESSON, PROFESSOR! ADAM NEEDS OUR HELP!
HOLD ON! I'VE GOT AN IDEA!

FZZZZNK
THWIP
IF MY BRAINSTORM FAILS, THIS PLACE IS GONNA BLOW UP LIKE MOUNT VESUVIUS!
WISH ME LUCK, GENTS.
BE CAREFUL, HOMME-- REMEMBER, HE'S JUST A BOY!
SPIDER-MAN...?
LISTEN TO ME, ADAM. IF I DIDN'T BRING YOU TO CONNORS' LAB, YOU'D BE OKAY RIGHT NOW. I'M SORRY, BUT--
--HOW 'BOUT GIVIN' ME ANOTHER CHANCE? LET ME TRY TO MAKE IT UP TO YOU. LET ME TRY TO HELP...
...PLEASE.
I KNOW YOU THINK EVERYBODY HATES YOU JUST BECAUSE YOU'RE DIFFERENT, RIGHT? THAT'S WHAT SINISTER WANTED YOU TO BELIEVE, BUT IT'S NOT TRUE...
IT'S JUST THAT MOST PEOPLE DON'T UNDERSTAND SOMEONE WHO'S DIFFERENT, AND IT FRIGHTENS THEM.
I UNDERSTAND, ADAM. SO DO GUYS LIKE THE X-MEN. WE'RE JUST LIKE YOU. WE KNOW WHAT IT'S LIKE TO BE DIFFERENT...
DON'T PUSH TOO HARD, SPIDEY... ONE WRONG MOVE WILL MESS UP THIS KID FOR LIFE!
OUR DIFFERENCES MAKE US SPECIAL. LOOK AT ME...
FZZZ
ZZK
KRAKL
I'VE BEEN PLACES AND MET PEOPLE YOU WOULDN'T BELIEVE! I FOUGHT ALONGSIDE THE FANTASTIC FOUR AND THE AVENGERS IN AN INTERGALACTIC WAR...
...BATTLED DR. DOOM, VENOM, AND THE LIZARD ALL OVER THE WORLD!
PRETTY COOL, HUH?
ALL BECAUSE I AM DIFFERENT.

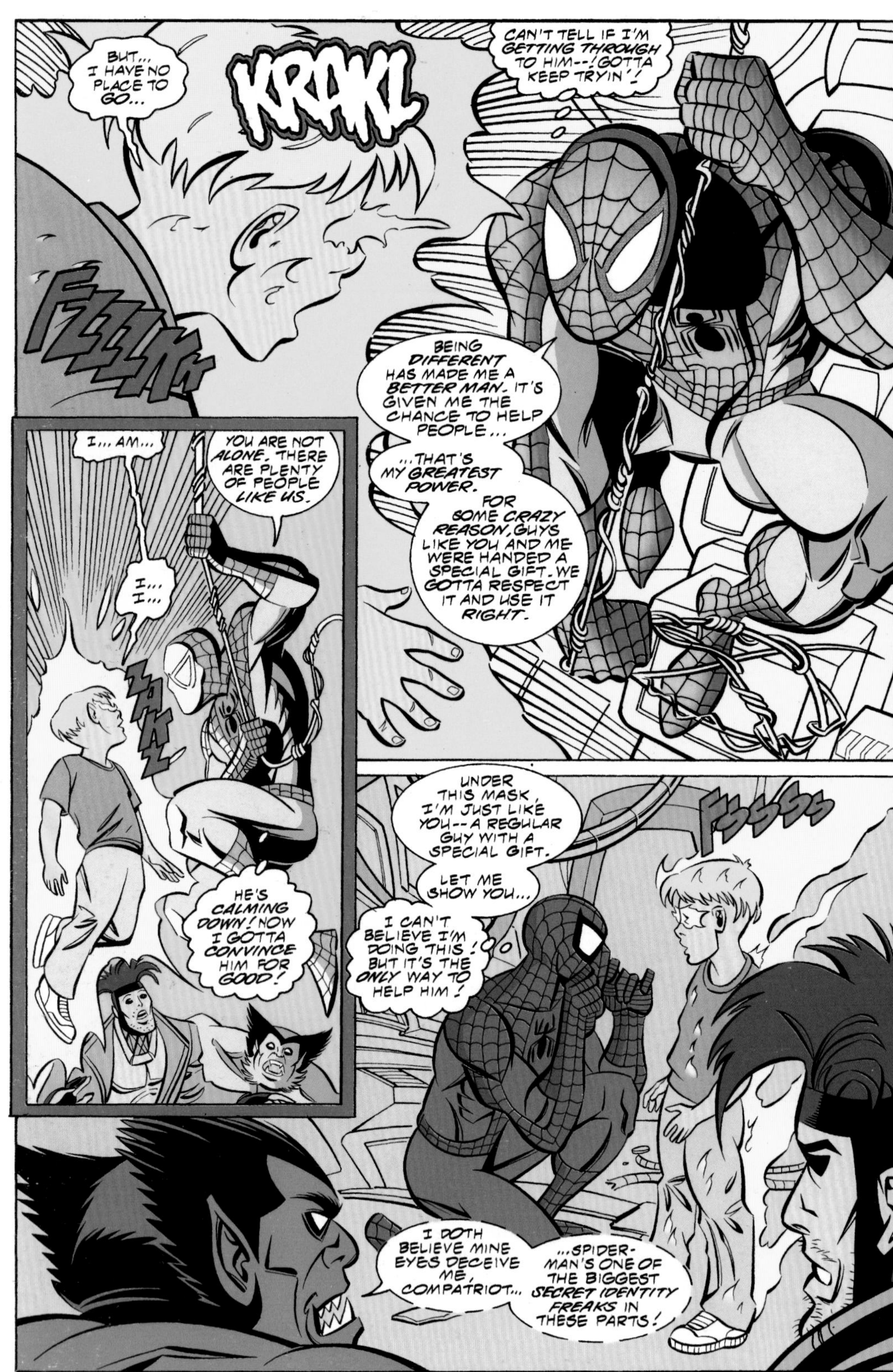
BUT... I HAVE NO PLACE TO GO...
KRAK!
CAN'T TELL IF I'M GETTING THROUGH TO HIM--! GOTTA KEEP TRYIN'!
FZZZAKK
BEING DIFFERENT HAS MADE ME A BETTER MAN. IT'S GIVEN ME THE CHANCE TO HELP PEOPLE...
...THAT'S MY GREATEST POWER.
FOR SOME CRAZY REASON, GUYS LIKE YOU AND ME WERE HANDED A SPECIAL GIFT. WE GOTTA RESPECT IT AND USE IT RIGHT.
I... AM...
YOU ARE NOT ALONE. THERE ARE PLENTY OF PEOPLE LIKE US.
I... I...
ZAKZ
HE'S CALMING DOWN! NOW I GOTTA CONVINCE HIM FOR GOOD!
UNDER THIS MASK, I'M JUST LIKE YOU-- A REGULAR GUY WITH A SPECIAL GIFT.
LET ME SHOW YOU...
FSSSS
I CAN'T BELIEVE I'M DOING THIS! BUT IT'S THE ONLY WAY TO HELP HIM!
I DOTH BELIEVE MINE EYES DECEIVE ME, COMPATRIOT...
...SPIDER-MAN'S ONE OF THE BIGGEST SECRET IDENTITY FREAKS IN THESE PARTS!

YOU'LL SEE THAT UNDER THIS FOREBODING MASK OF SPANDEX LIES THE SWEET, LOVABLE VISAGE OF AN EVERYDAY JOE!
UNF! HERE IT COMES...

I...I...
KRRRR

WANNA WARN YA, THOUGH... NOT ONLY HAVEN'T I SHAVED LATELY, BUT THIS THING GIVES ME THE WORST HAIR DAYS YOU CAN IMAGINE!

I...I...
S-SPIDER-MAN...

...NO! YOU DON'T HAVE TO DO THAT!
I DON'T CARE WHAT YOU LOOK LIKE...
HUH--?

...I KNOW BY WHAT YOU SAID THAT YOU THINK LIKE ME... IF WE THINK THE SAME, THEN I KNOW YOU UNDERSTAND ME.
I DON'T FEEL ALONE AND ANGRY ANYMORE.
I'M VERY PROUD OF YOU, ADAM. YOU'RE QUITE A SPECIAL BOY.
AND DIS SPIDER-HOMME IS ONE SPECIAL KIND O' SUPER HERO, eh, MON AMI?
YOU'LL GET NO ARGUMENT FROM THE BOUNDING BEAST ON THAT OBSERVATION, SPIKE!

NOW, TEAM, HERE'S THE MILLION DOLLAR QUESTION-- WHAT HAPPENS TO ADAM?
I T'INK THE COURTS WILL MAYBE DECIDE DAT FOR US.
I'LL SAVE THEM THE TROUBLE. I WANT TO GO BACK TO THE ORPHANAGE. I BELONG WITH THE OTHER KIDS.
EITHER YOU MAKE A JOKE, ME BOYO, OR YOU'VE FORGOTTEN THAT THOSE SELFSAME YOUTH CAUSED YOU GRIEVOUS HARM!
THEY'VE DISPLAYED NO UNDERSTANDING OF YOU, ADAM!
THEN I HAVE TO MAKE THEM UNDERSTAND. I'VE GOTTA TEACH THEM THAT BEING DIFFERENT IS NO REASON TO HATE OR FEAR.
I'LL BE FINE, GUYS... DON'T WORRY.
IT WON'T BE EASY, MON PETIT.
HE'LL HAVE US TO HELP HIM OVER THE ROUGH SPOTS, GAMBIT.
WHAT ABOUT YOU, SPIDER-MAN? WON'T I EVER SEE YOU AGAIN?
WILD HORSES COULDN'T KEEP ME AWAY, KID!
BESIDES, I OWE YOU ONE...
...I'D HATE TO THINK WHAT WOULD HAPPEN IF THE WHOLE WORLD KNEW I WAS PETER PARKER!
DON'T BE STRANGERS, X-MEN... I'M IN THE PHONE BOOK! SEE YA 'ROUND, FELLAS!
NEXT ISSUE:
FLYIN' THE UNFRIENDLY SKIES WITH--THE VULTURE!

MARVEL COMICS
NEW STORIES BASED ON THE HIT TV SHOW!
APPROVED BY THE COMICS CODE AUTHORITY
THE ADVENTURES OF SPIDER-MAN
SPIDER-MAN
JULY '96 4
ONLY 99¢
THE VULTURE'S PREY!
KUHN

BITTEN BY A RADIOACTIVE SPIDER, COLLEGE STUDENT ***PETER PARKER*** GAINED THE PROPORTIONATE STRENGTH AND AGILITY OF A SPIDER! ARMED WITH HIS WONDROUS WEB-SHOOTERS AND COMMITTED TO USING HIS AMAZING POWERS FOR GOOD, HE STRUGGLES WITH SINISTER SUPER-VILLAINS, MAKING ENDS MEET, AND MAINTAINING SOME SEMBLANCE OF A NORMAL LIFE!

HERE NOW, BASED ON HIS ANIMATED TELEVISION SERIES, ARE... THE ADVENTURES OF SPIDER-MAN

THE VULTURE'S RAGE

NEL YOMTOV	ALEX SAVIUK	ROB STULL	KEVIN TINSLEY	STEVE DUTRO	MALIBU COMPUTER COLOR	MARK POWERS	BOB HARRAS
WRITER	PENCILER	INKER	COLORIST	LETTERER	COLOR	EDITOR	EDITOR IN CHIEF

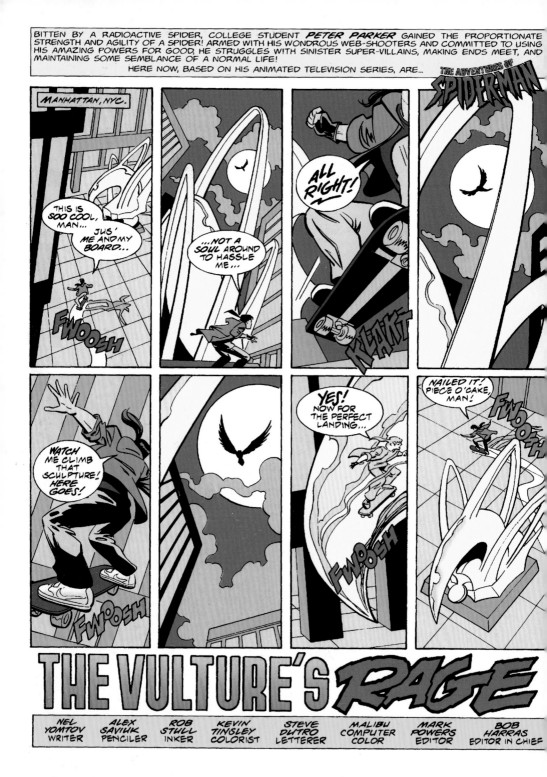

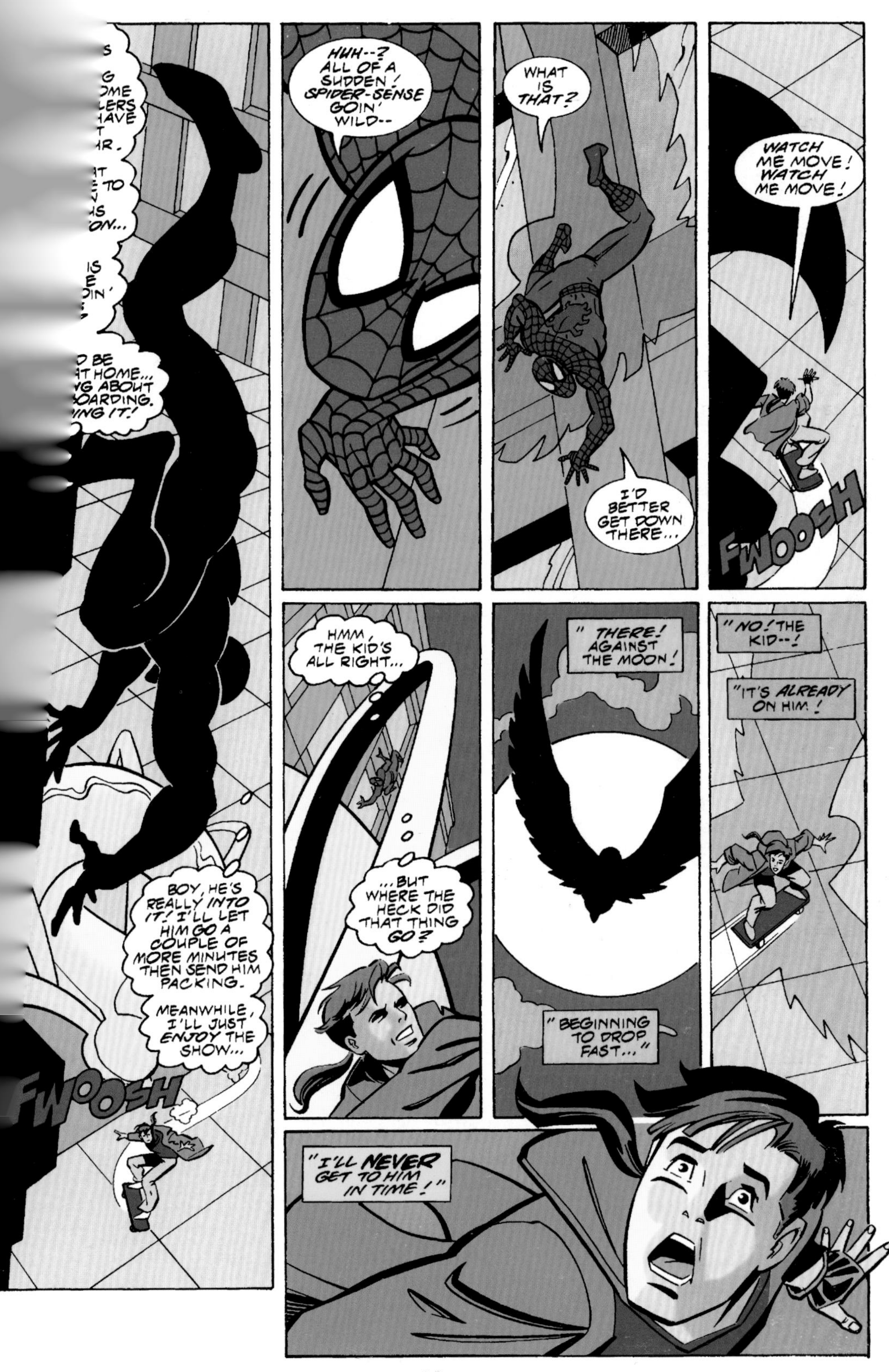
BOY, HE'S REALLY INTO IT! I'LL LET HIM GO A COUPLE OF MORE MINUTES THEN SEND HIM PACKING.
MEANWHILE, I'LL JUST ENJOY THE SHOW...
FWOOSH
HUH--? ALL OF A SUDDEN! SPIDER-SENSE GOIN' WILD--
WHAT IS THAT?
I'D BETTER GET DOWN THERE...
WATCH ME MOVE! WATCH ME MOVE!
FWOOSH
HMM, THE KID'S ALL RIGHT...
...BUT WHERE THE HECK DID THAT THING GO?
"THERE! AGAINST THE MOON!
"BEGINNING TO DROP FAST..."
"NO! THE KID--!
"IT'S ALREADY ON HIM!
"I'LL NEVER GET TO HIM IN TIME!"

NOOO!
STAYING OUT LATE TONIGHT, BOY?
HAVEN'T YOU BEEN WARNED OF THE DANGERS THAT CAN BEFALL YOU AT THIS HOUR?
YOUNG FOOL...
AIEEE!
DARING TO TEST YOUR OWN MORTALITY! YOU ARE BLINDED BY THE ARROGANCE OF YOUR LEAN YEARS!
DO YOU THINK YOURSELF ETERNALLY YOUNG? ETERNALLY STRONG AND VIBRANT?!
NO, YOU ARE NOT...
BUT ME...
THABATHOOM
SHTOOMB
YES! YES!
YES!
IT WORKS! I'VE DONE IT! I'VE--
HATE TO BREAK UP YOUR SOLILOQUY, SHAKESPEARE, BUT IT'S GONNA HAVE TO WAIT--
EAGHH!!
SHTOOMB
--UNTIL AFTER INTERMISSION TIME!

AND THAT'S NOT GONNA BE FOR A LOOOONG TIME, YOU WINGED CREEP!
BY THE WAY, TRY TO KEEP THE MOLTING TO A MINIMUM, OKAY?
UNNGH!
FWACK
POOR KID. I SHOULD'VE SEEN THE ATTACK COMING...
...WHY DIDN'T I MOVE FASTER TO HELP HIM?!
IF ANYTHING BAD HAS HAPPENED--
WHA--?!
WHAT IN THE NAME OF --?!
OH, NO!
GET AWAY FROM HIM, SPIDER-MAN! THIS IS NONE OF YOUR CONCERN!
TURNING A HEALTHY YOUNG BOY INTO A DROOLING GERIATRIC IS EXACTLY MY CONCERN, FLYBOY!
MORPH HIM BACK OR I SWEAR I'LL--
WHOOSH

YES? AND WHAT MAKES YOU THINK THAT MORPHING HIM BACK IS EVEN A REMOTE POSSIBILITY?
WHAT IF HIS CONDITION IS... PERMANENT?
HOW WILL YOU FEEL KNOWING THAT YOU WERE RESPONSIBLE FOR THE BOY'S HORRID FATE?
Y-YOU'RE CRAZY, BIRDMAN... H-HE'LL BE ALL RIGHT...
YOU PRESUME FAR TOO MUCH, WEB-SLINGER!
BTANG
WHOA! HIS WINGS SLICED THROUGH THAT LAMP POLE LIKE A HOT KNIFE THROUGH BUTTER!
CAN'T LET IT FALL ON THE KID--!
GOT IT! TOO BAD THERE ISN'T A METS SCOUT AROUND TO SEE THAT GRAB...
...I HEAR THEY COULD USE SOME OUTFIELD HELP THIS YEAR!
UNFORTUNATELY, YOUR FUTURE ISN'T AS ROSY AS THEIRS, SPIDER-MAN!
JUST HOW LONG DO YOU THINK YOU CAN PROTECT YOUR OWN LIFE--
--AND THAT OF THE HELPLESS OLD MAN?
SPEAKING OF THINGS OLD AND NEW...

...DID YOU KNOW HOW MUCH I HATED MODERN ART?!
SUCH A SENSELESS WASTE OF ONE'S PRECIOUS TIME, NO?
SHRANG
TONS OF FALLING STEEL!
HOPE YOU BROUGHT AN UMBRELLA, WEB-SLINGER...
...I HEAR IT RAINS HEAVY METAL THIS TIME OF YEAR!
SHUNG
NO! HE'LL BE CRUSHED IF I DON'T REACH HIM IN TIME!
I... DID IT... I SAVED HIM. ACTED QUICKLY ENOUGH... THIS TIME...
UNNHGH! FEELS LIKE... I JUST WENT FIFTEEN ROUNDS... WITH THE HULK... SO WEAK...
I WARNED YOU THAT THIS WAS NONE OF YOUR BUSINESS.
NOW YOU WILL DIE AT THE HANDS OF... THE VULTURE!
ARISE AND--
RNNNNNN
WHA--? WHAT'S GOING ON? WHAT'S HAPPENING TO ME?

N-NO! NO! NOOO!
THE EFFECT... NOT LONG ENOUGH...
IT LASTED ONLY TWO MINUTES! NEED MORE TIME...!
THAB-
ATHOOOM
I MUST LEAVE--RETURN LATER TO COMPLETE MY MISSION... WITHOUT SPIDER-MAN'S INTERFERENCE...
FORGET IT, VULTURE! FROM HERE ON IN, I'M YOUR SHADOW-- I'M GONNA BE ALL OVER YOU LIKE A BAD DREAM!
YOU'RE GONNA PAY FOR WHAT YOU DID TO THIS KID!
RNNNNN
THE KID--!
HUH? GOOD LORD!
HE'S OKAY! NOT A WRINKLE OR A GRAY HAIR ON 'IM!
AS FOR THE VULTURE...
...HE'S LONG GONE. NO WAY I CAN CATCH HIM.
I WONDER WHAT HE MEANT ABOUT "COMPLETING HIS MISSION."
SOME-THING TELLS ME THINGS ARE GONNA GET REAL UGLY AROUND HERE...

MEANWHILE, AT THE CORPORATE HEAD-QUARTERS OF OSCORP INTERNATIONAL...

...AND IF TOOMES AERODYNAMICS IS ALLOWED TO CONTINUE ON ITS PRESENT COURSE OF SELF-DESTRUCTION, YOUR COMPANY WILL BE FINANCIALLY RUINED.

LET ME TELL YOU, DIRECTORS OF THE BOARD, HOW YOUR COMPANY'S PROFITS ARE BEING SQUANDERED ON THE OLD MAN'S SECRET PET PROJECTS...

I HAVE HERE SOME FILES--

OSBORN! IF HIS PROJECTS ARE SO SECRETIVE, HOW'VE YOU COME INTO POSSESSION OF THOSE REPORTS?

THAT'S NOT IMPORTANT, MR. DEAN. WHAT YOU SHOULD BE CONCERNED ABOUT IS WHERE YOUR PROFITS ARE BEING CHANNELED...

LOOK AT THESE...

TOP SECRET

AGE REVERSAL STUDIES

TOP SECRET

ANTI-GRAVIT FINDIN

IS THIS WHERE YOU WANT YOUR MONEY TO BE SPENT? HE'S LOST TOUCH WITH REALITY, I TELL YOU!

WHAT'S YOUR INTEREST IN TOOMES AERODYNAMICS, OSBORN? WHY SHOULD YOU CARE WHAT HAPPENS TO OUR COMPANY?
AS AN AMERICAN ENTREPRENEUR, MR. LYONS, I CARE ABOUT THE FATE OF ALL OUR NATION'S INDUSTRIES...
GENTLEMEN, I APPEAL TO YOUR SENSE OF PRESERVING A WAY OF LIFE... OUR WAY OF LIFE...

...LET ME BUY TOOMES AERODYNAMICS, FOLD IT INTO OSCORP INTER-NATIONAL AND INCREASE PROFITS. I PROMISE...
...YOU WILL ALL BECOME RICHER THAN YOU EVER IMAGINED!

HOLD ON A SECOND, OSBORN. WE KNOW THE OLD MAN SOMETIMES DOES FOOLISH THINGS, BUT HE'S THE FOUNDER OF THE COMPANY!
HE'S NEARLY WORKED HIMSELF TO DEATH TO KEEP IT AFLOAT!
TRUE, BUT YOU'VE GOT TO FACE THE INEVITABLE, PICKETT! HE'S SIMPLY BECOME TOO OLD AND FEEBLE TO LEAD THIS COMPANY IN A MODERN AGE!
WHO KNOWS WHAT KIND OF IRREVERSIBLE DAMAGE HE CAN DO WHILE HE REMAINS IN CHARGE?!
OSBORN'S GOT A POINT...OR HAVE YOU ALL FORGOTTEN HOW THE OLD MAN BUNGLED THE GOVERNMENT CONTRACT FOR THE UNDERSIDE SENSORS?
WE'LL NEVER BE CONTRACTED BY UNCLE SAM AGAIN!
THAT'S RIGHT! AND WASN'T IT HIS IDEA TO CANCEL RESEARCH ON THE VOICE ACTIVATION CHIP?
WE HAVE NOTHING TO SHOW FOR THE MILLIONS WE SPENT ON DEVELOPMENT!
YESTERDAY HE BLASTED ME FOR NOT TURNING IN THE JENKINS FIGURES.
I PERSONALLY GAVE THEM TO HIM LAST WEEK! HE MUST BE GOING SENILE...!
YES, IT'S UNFORTUNATE. HE WAS ONCE A PIONEER OF FLIGHT TECHNOLOGY. SADLY, HIS OLD AGE--
WE JUST CAN'T KICK HIM OUT! WE'RE NOT CRUEL MEN, OSBORN.
OF COURSE NOT. HE'LL LEAVE WITH A TIDY FINANCIAL PACKAGE TO PURSUE HIS "RESEARCH!"
WITH THAT NOW SETTLED, GENTLEMEN, I ASSUME WE HAVE AN UNDER-STANDING...
...I WILL RETURN TOOMES AERODYNAMICS TO ITS RIGHTFUL PLACE IN THE WORLD MARKET AND YOU WILL END THE INCOMPETENT PRESIDENCY OF--

--ADRIAN TOOMES!
FOREST HILLS, QUEENS, THE NEXT MORNING...
I DIDN'T KNOW HE WAS STILL RUNNING HIS BUSINESS. HE'S ONE OLD-TIMER WHO SURE DOESN'T KNOW WHEN TO CALL IT QUITS!
I THINK IT'S KINDA CUTE THAT HE GOES TO WORK EVERY DAY, AFTER ALL THESE YEARS!
WHAT DOES THE PAPER SAY ABOUT HIM, PETER DEAR?
METS DO IT
NOT A LOT OF GOOD THINGS, AUNT MAY. LOOKS LIKE HE'S FALLEN ON HARD TIMES...
...ANALYSTS SAY THAT TOOMES'S FAILURE TO MODERNIZE HAVE COST HIM BIG MONEY... PROFITS ARE DOWN... STOCK-HOLDERS ARE UPSET...
...THE BOARD OF DIRECTORS IS BEGINNING TO GRUMBLE. THERE ARE RUMORED REPORTS OF WASTEFUL SPENDING ON DEAD END RESEARCH...
THE CLINCHER IS THAT NORMAN OSBORN MAY BE MAKING AN AGGRESSIVE BID TO GET THE OLD MAN DUMPED SO THAT HE CAN BUY OUT THE COMPANY!
HARRY'S DAD? I KNOW HE'S YOUR BEST PAL, PETEY, BUT HIS DAD HAS BEEN INVOLVED IN MORE SHADY DEALS THAN I CAN COUNT!
DIDN'T I READ SOMEWHERE THAT HE WORKED WITH KINGPIN AND THE HOBGOBLIN TO KILL SPIDER-MAN?
DAILY BUGLE
TOOMES AERO REPORTS RECORD LOSSES
ONE TIME GIANT FORCED TO DOWNSIZE-TALKS OF TAKEOVER BY OSCORP INTERNATIONAL
I-I DON'T KNOW ANYTHING ABOUT SPIDER-MAN, MJ, BUT TRYING TO BOOT OUT POOR TOOMES IS PRETTY NASTY!
I BET IT ALL HAS TO DO WITH TOOMES'S AGE! SOMEBODY OUGHT TO SET OL' NORMIE STRAIGHT!
AND I KNOW JUST THE PERFECT WALL-CRAWLER TO DO IT!
YEAH! OLD PEOPLE IN THIS COUNTRY GET SUCH A RAW DEAL! SHOVED ASIDE AND FORGOTTEN LIKE USED FURNITURE!
SOCIAL SECURITY BARELY KEEPS THEM FED. NOBODY WILL HIRE THEM, THEY GET DUMPED IN OLD AGE HOMES--
WELL, THAT MAY BE, MARY JANE, BUT--

IN CHINA, OLD PEOPLE ARE TREATED LIKE ROYALTY! THEY'RE VALUED FOR THEIR EXPERIENCE AND WISDOM! WHY CAN'T IT BE THAT WAY HERE?
IT'S BECAUSE WE HAVE NO RESPECT FOR THOSE QUALITIES! OLD PEOPLE IN AMERICA ARE LIKE DISPOSABLE LIGHTERS-- YOU GET USED UP AND YOU'RE THROWN AWAY!
NO ONE CARES ABOUT TOOMES'S FEELINGS! NO ONE CARES HOW THIS TAKEOVER WILL CRUSH HIS SPIRIT--
HOLD ON, YOU TWO...
YOU'RE NOT GIVING ELDERLY FOLKS ANY CREDIT IF YOU THINK THAT WE JUMP INTO A PIT OF DESPAIR AND HOPELESS-NESS AS WE GET OLD AND HAVE TO FACE ADVERSITY.
AGING HAPPENS TO EVERYONE, BUT WHAT'S IMPORTANT, CHILDREN, IS HOW YOU DEAL WITH IT.
B-BUT--
I WASN'T EXACTLY A YOUNG WOMAN WHEN MY HUSBAND BEN DIED, Y'KNOW. SURELY, HIS MURDER DEVASTATED ME, BUT I DIDN'T GROW BITTER AND GIVE UP.
NO, I PULLED MY LIFE TOGETHER AND GOT ON WITH THINGS. ISN'T THAT RIGHT, PETER?
YOUR AUNT ANNA HAS HAD MANY SERIOUS AILMENTS AS SHE'S GOTTEN OLDER, MARY JANE, BUT SHE'S STILL AS CHEERFUL AND VIBRANT AS THE DAY I MET HER ALL THOSE YEARS AGO!
DO YOU SEE MY POINT?
YOU'VE GOT TO TURN YOUR OLD AGE INTO "GOLDEN YEARS" BY USING YOUR HARD-WON WISDOM AND PUTTING THE KNOCKS OF EXPERIENCE TO WORK FOR YOU.
PEOPLE MAKE THEIR OWN CHOICES-- YOU EITHER ACCEPT GROWING OLD AND LIVE HAPPILY OR DENY THE INEVITABLE AND BE RESENTFUL AND BITTER.
I CHOSE TO REAFFIRM LIFE BECAUSE PARKERS AREN'T QUITTERS-- WE NEVER GIVE UP!
YOUR MR. TOOMES HAS THE SAME CHOICE ALL OLD PEOPLE DO. HOW HE REACTS IS STRICTLY UP TO HIM.
MARK MY WORDS, HE'LL DO WHATEVER COMES NATURALLY TO HIM...

THAT NIGHT. TOOMES AERODYNAMICS...
...NO NO NO!
HE'LL NOT STEAL WHAT I'VE TAKEN YEARS TO BUILD AND NURTURE!
HE PLAYS ME FOR AN UNWITTING OLD FOOL, BUT I KNOW OF HIS TREACHERY AND THE CLANDESTINE MEETINGS WITH THE DIRECTORS OF THE TOOMES BOARD!
I KNOW HOW HE TRIES TO PUBLICLY DESTROY ME BY LEAKING MY CONFIDENTIAL FINANCIAL STATEMENTS TO THE PRESS!
I KNOW HOW HE MOCKS MY RESEARCH, WRITING IT OFF AS NO MORE THAN THE EXCESSES OF ADVANCED SENILITY!
NO...
NORMAN OSBORN IS THE TRUE FOOL IF HE THINKS HE CAN TAKE MY COMPANY--MY VERY LIFE--AWAY FROM ME.
I'VE LOST MUCH TO THE YEARS, BUT NOT THIS. YES, I HAVE LOST MUCH...
"STRENGTH. ENDURANCE. ATHLETIC PROWESS. I HAD THEM ALL. OTHERS WERE RELUCTANT TO COMPETE WITH ME...
"...ON THE TOOMES ASSEMBLY LINE, I PROVED WHAT A RIGOROUS MAN WITH DRIVE WAS CAPABLE OF ACHIEVING.
"NO ONE COULD MATCH MY RAZOR-SHARP INTELLECT, DAZZLING EVEN THE MOST EDUCATED MINDS..."
"BEAUTIFUL WOMEN FLOCKED TO BE AROUND MY GOOD LOOKS AND GRACEFULNESS. I HAD MY PICK OF THE LITTER.

NOW THESE ARE NO MORE THAN SOURED MEMORIES. THE RAVAGES OF TIME HAVE ROBBED ME OF NEARLY EVERYTHING.
ALL I'VE BEEN LEFT WITH IS MY WORK... BUT OSBORN UNDERESTIMATES ME IF HE THINKS I WILL NOT FIGHT WITH ALL THAT IS IN ME TO KEEP IT.
IT IS THE LAST MISTAKE HE WILL EVER MAKE.
AND THIS TIME, MR. NORMAN OSBORN--
--THERE WILL BE NO UNPLANNED INTERRUPTIONS BY SPIDER-MAN TO DETER ME FROM MY MISSION!
TONIGHT, YOU BLOOD-SUCKING ROBBER BARON--
--YOU WILL DIE BY THE VERY TECHNOLOGY YOU MOCK!
TONIGHT YOU WILL TASTE THE RAGE OF THE VULTURE!
WHOOOSH

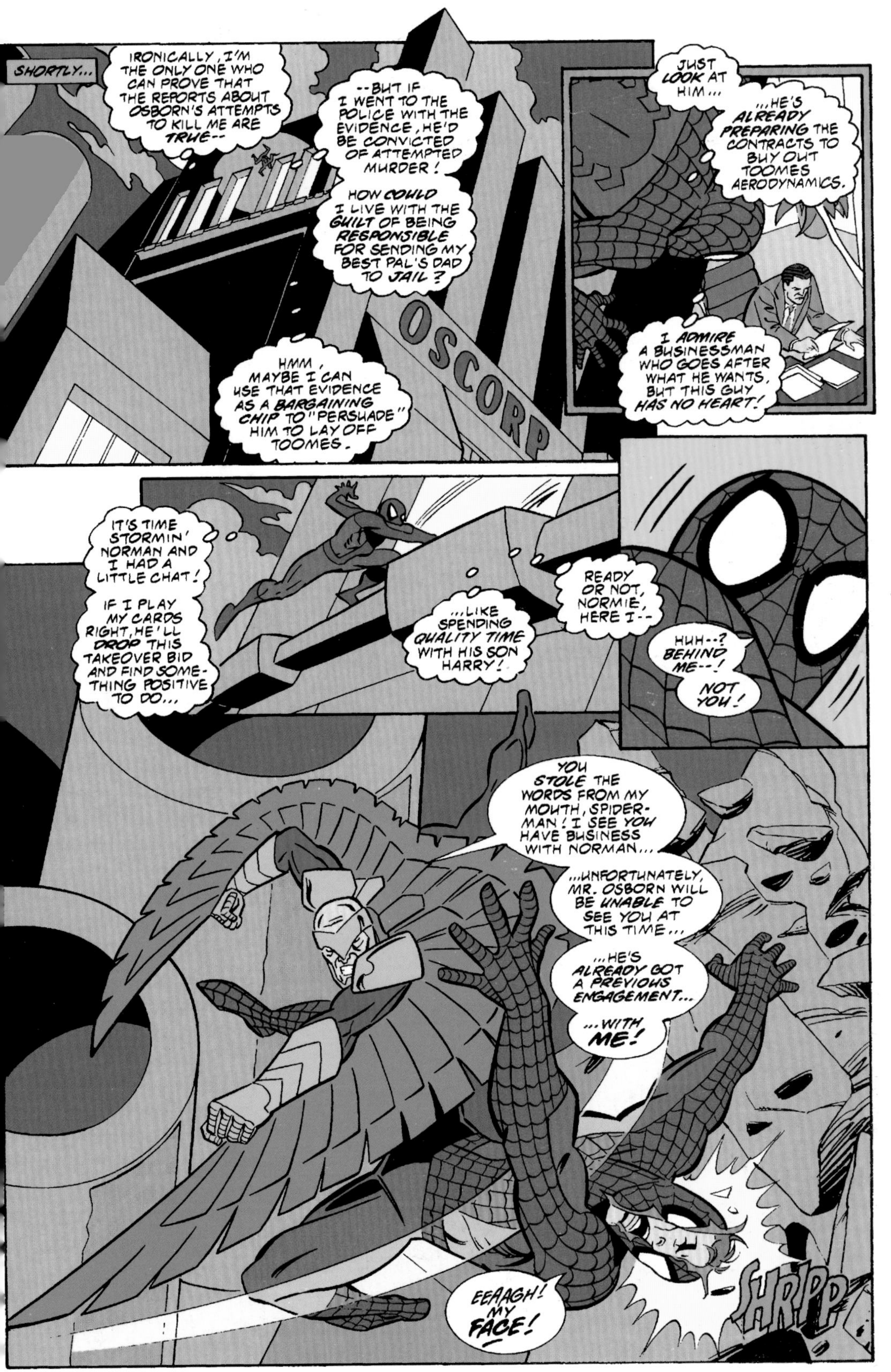
SHORTLY...
IRONICALLY, I'M THE ONLY ONE WHO CAN PROVE THAT THE REPORTS ABOUT OSBORN'S ATTEMPTS TO KILL ME ARE TRUE--
--BUT IF I WENT TO THE POLICE WITH THE EVIDENCE, HE'D BE CONVICTED OF ATTEMPTED MURDER!
HOW COULD I LIVE WITH THE GUILT OF BEING RESPONSIBLE FOR SENDING MY BEST PAL'S DAD TO JAIL?
OSCORP
HMM, MAYBE I CAN USE THAT EVIDENCE AS A BARGAINING CHIP TO "PERSUADE" HIM TO LAY OFF TOOMES.
JUST LOOK AT HIM...
...HE'S ALREADY PREPARING THE CONTRACTS TO BUY OUT TOOMES AERODYNAMICS.
I ADMIRE A BUSINESSMAN WHO GOES AFTER WHAT HE WANTS, BUT THIS GUY HAS NO HEART!
IT'S TIME STORMIN' NORMAN AND I HAD A LITTLE CHAT!
IF I PLAY MY CARDS RIGHT, HE'LL DROP THIS TAKEOVER BID AND FIND SOME-THING POSITIVE TO DO...
...LIKE SPENDING QUALITY TIME WITH HIS SON HARRY!
READY OR NOT, NORMIE, HERE I--
HUH--? BEHIND ME--!
NOT YOU!
YOU STOLE THE WORDS FROM MY MOUTH, SPIDER-MAN! I SEE YOU HAVE BUSINESS WITH NORMAN...
...UNFORTUNATELY, MR. OSBORN WILL BE UNABLE TO SEE YOU AT THIS TIME...
...HE'S ALREADY GOT A PREVIOUS ENGAGEMENT...
...WITH ME!
SHRIPP
EEAAGH! MY FACE!

THAT'S NOTHING COMPARED TO WHAT I'M ABOUT TO DO, FOOL!
I CAN'T BELIEVE IT! HE'S COMIN' IN FOR A MID-AIR KILL!
GOTTA GET OUT OF HIS PATH--! BREAK MY FALL--! GOTTA DO SOMETHING!
THERE! THAT BUILDING! ONLY ONE CHANCE--!
TH-
SLICE
WIP!
NO
GUHKK!
WHAKPT
KAVABOOOM!
EAARHH!

MOMENTARILY...
MY ATTACK HAS SEEMINGLY MADE ME THE VICTOR, SPIDER-MAN, BUT AS SOMEONE OF BOTH INTELLECT AND PRACTICAL-ITY--
--I CONCEDE THAT A MAN OF MY YEARS HAS NO HOPE OF DEFEATING ONE AS YOUTHFUL AND INDESTRUCT-IBLE AS YOU.
LIKE OSBORN, YOU THINK I'M A CRAZY OLD MAN. IRRATIONAL. IRRESPONSIBLE. DIRECTIONLESS. YOU ARE BOTH GRAVELY MISTAKEN...
BEFORE I "REMEDY" THIS UNJUST IMBALANCE I WANT TO SHARE WITH YOU SOMETHING THAT YOUR FERTILE YOUNG MIND MAY APPRECIATE-- WHILE IT STILL CAN.
"..I SAW OLD AGE FOR WHAT IT WAS... BARREN AND MEANINGLESS... WAITING FOR DEATH'S VISIT IN COMPLACENT IDLENESS...
"...I WANTED TO BE YOUNG FOREVER! AS A MAN OF SCIENCE, I HAD TO FIND A WAY TO DO IT!
" I LABORED LONG HOURS IN SECRECY, BRINGING TO LIFE ANCIENT TECHNOLO-GIES AND CONQUERING THE VERY FORCE OF GRAVITY ITSELF...
"... FINALLY, MY LABORS WERE REWARDED WITH SUCCESS! I REALIZED MY DREAM OF POSSESSING ETERNAL YOUTH!
YOU KNOW MINE AREN'T THE RAVINGS OF A MADMAN! YOU WITNESSED PROOF OF MY POWERS LAST NIGHT WHEN I OVERCAME THE SKATEBOARDER!
I WAS EN ROUTE TO DEAL WITH MR. OSBORN WHEN YOU SHOWED UP. YESTERDAY, HE WAS MERELY GOING TO DIE BY THE LIFE ENERGY OF THAT YOUTH...
...BUT TONIGHT, BECAUSE OF YOUR UNFORTUITOUS MEDDLING, HE WILL DIE BY THE POWER OF ONE BLESSED WITH THE PROPORTION-ATE STRENGTH OF A SPIDER!
NOW, SPIDER-MAN, I WANT WHAT YOU HAVE!

GIVE IT TO ME!
THABATHOOOM!

VULTURE...
...TOOMES...
...NO...
RNNNNNNNNNNNNNN
YES! LOOK WHO THE OLD MAN NOW, SPIDER-MAN!
YOU'RE PATHETIC! OLD! WITHERED! NOW YOU KNOW THE PAIN WHICH I'VE SUFFERED THROUGH! BUT NO MORE!
SOON I WILL MASTER THE SECRETS OF PERMANENTLY ASSUMING A YOUNG BODY. NO LONGER WILL IT BE NECESSARY FOR ME TO INHABIT MY OLD SELF...
...FACE IT, OLD FOOL, YOU ARE NOW THE HELPLESS ONE... YOU ARE WITHOUT HOPE, SPIDER-MAN...
...SO WEAK... BARELY CAN MOVE...

CAN'T LET HIM WIN... HE'LL KILL OSBORN!
MUST STOP HIM!

I'VE GOT TO GET FREE--NO MATTER HOW BAD THE ODDS ARE!
TRY TO--LIFT THIS--OFF ME!

I--MUST--DO IT--!

UNNGHH... I CAN'T! HAVE NO STRENGTH--MY BODY--SO OLD--SO WEAK--!

LAST NIGHT I HEARD VULTURE SAY THAT THE YOUTH TRANSFERENCE EFFECT LASTED TWO MINUTES. IF I DON'T GET FREE IN THAT TIME--I'LL BE CRUSHED!
I'VE GOT TO GET OUT--NOW! BUT HOW?
...AUNT MAY SAID SOMETHING... I REMEMBER...

ADMIRABLE, SPIDER-MAN... BUT FUTILE.
YOU'RE GOING TO DIE UNDER THAT WEIGHT, YOU DECREPIT OLD FOOL!
SAVE YOURSELF FOR THE AFTERLIFE! GIVE UP NOW!

PARKERS NEVER QUIT... AUNT MAY SAID PARKERS NEVER QUIT! I'VE GOT TO CALL ON ALL MY STRENGTH--USE EVERY-THING THAT I'VE GOT!
UNNGH! THE WEIGHT IS UNBEARABLE!
I CAN'T GIVE UP NOW! GOTTA KEEP TRYIN'!
I'LL DO IT, AUNT MAY! I'LL SHOW YOU THAT YOU'RE RIGHT! I WON'T LET YOU DOWN! I WON'T FAIL!
IT'S MOVING! GOT TO KEEP PUSHIN'! CAN'T LET UP! JUST A LITTLE MORE!
IT'S IMPOSSIBLE... THIS CAN'T BE--!
YESS! I DID IT! I'M FREE!
SKROOOOM!

CONGRATULATIONS, OLD-TIMER, BUT WHAT DO YOU PLAN TO DO NOW? YOU HARDLY HAVE THE STRENGTH TO LIFT YOUR ARMS!
PERHAPS, TOOMES, THAT'S ALL I REALLY HAVE TO DO...
GOTTA KEEP HIM AT BAY LONG ENOUGH FOR THE CHANGE TO TAKE PLACE! IT'S MY ONLY HOPE...
...IN MY CONDITION, ONE OF HIS PUNCHES WILL KILL ME!
THWUPP
DAMN YOU, OLD FOOL!
BARELY REACHED HIM WITH MY WEBBING! I GOT LUCKY, WITH THAT SHOT, BUT IF HE RECOVERS...
UNNGH!
WHEN IS THE TRANSFORMATION GONNA HAPPEN? I CAN'T HOLD HIM OFF MUCH LONGER! CAN'T KEEP HIM OFF BALANCE FOREVER!
JUST GOTTA THROW MYSELF AT HIM!
THERE!
SLAMM!
HE'LL BE ON ME IN SECONDS! BUT... I CAN'T... MOVE! TOO WEAK... CHEST POUNDING... FEELS LIKE A... HEART ATTACK!

TOO BAD TOOMES NEVER SAW HOW ALL HIS KNOWLEDGE AND EXPERIENCE COULD HAVE MADE HIM A WINNER.

SO NOW, INSTEAD OF ENJOYING HIS GOLDEN YEARS, HE'LL ROT AWAY IN A LONELY JAIL CELL. ALONE WITH HIS BITTER, ANGRY THOUGHTS...

...AND WHEN HE GETS OUT, HE WON'T EVEN HAVE WHAT HE FOUGHT SO DESPERATELY TO KEEP--TOOMES AERODYNAMICS. NO, OSBORN WILL GRAB THE COMPANY AND SUCK IT DRY...

LIVES AND DREAMS WILL BE BROKEN. EVERYBODY LOSES, OSBORN MAKES SOME FAST CASH. SOMETIMES LIFE REALLY STINKS...

...BUT I'VE LEARNED THAT IF I WANT TO BE A PART OF MAKIN' THINGS A LITTLE BETTER, I HAVE TO KEEP MAKIN' THE RIGHT CHOICES AND DOIN' THE POSITIVE THINGS JUST LIKE AUNT MAY SAID...

...TIME TO PUT IN A 911 CALL TO NEW YORK'S FINEST AND LET THEM WRAP IT UP HERE. THEN IT'S BACK HOME FOR ME...

LATER, AFTER A TYPICALLY NOT-SO-QUICK SUBWAY RIDE FROM THE TURBULENCE OF MANHATTAN TO THE CALM OF FOREST HILLS...
HEY, LISTEN TO THIS!
WHO WANTS SOMETHIN' TO DRINK?
WHERE'S THE FOOD? WHERE'S THE FOOD?
WHAT'S ALL THAT NOISE COMIN' FROM THE HOUSE? IF ANYTHING HAS HAPPENED TO AUNT MAY WHILE I WAS OUT CHASIN' THE VULTURE--
OH, PETER, I WAS HOPING YOU'D GET HERE IN TIME!
IN TIME FOR WHAT? I HEARD THE RACKET FROM DOWN THE BLOCK AND I GOT HERE AS FAST AS I COULD! WHAT'S WRONG?
NOTHING'S WRONG, DEAR, BUT AFTER THE LITTLE TALK THIS MORNING WITH MARY JANE--
--I THOUGHT IT WOULD BE NICE TO HAVE SOME OF MY "ELDERLY" FRIENDS OVER FOR A PARTY!
HI, LOVER! COME ON IN AND JOIN THE FUN! YOU COULD LEARN A THING OR TWO ABOUT LOOSENING UP FROM MAY'S PALS!
M-MARY JANE? HERE? PARTYING WITH THE GERIATRIC GENERATION?!
NOW I'VE SEEN EVERY-THING!
GO AHEAD AND HAVE FUN TEASING OLD-TIMERS, PETER, BUT YOU HAVE NO IDEA WHAT US OLD FOLKS ARE CAPABLE OF WHEN WE PUT OUR MINDS TO IT!
DON'T BET ON IT, FAVORITE LADY O' MINE...
...I HAPPEN TO KNOW EXACTLY WHAT AN ELDERLY PERSON CAN DO WHEN THE CHIPS ARE DOWN! DON'T ASK ME HOW, BUT BELIEVE ME... I KNOW, I KNOW...
NEXT ISSUE: THE RHINO RULES!

MARVEL COMICS
NEW STORIE BASED ON THE HIT
TV SHOW!
THE A ENTURES OF
SP ER-MAN
SPIDER-MAN
AUG '96 5
ONLY 99¢
RHINO STAMPEDE!
KUHN

ITTEN BY A RADIOACTIVE SPIDER, COLLEGE STUDENT ***PETER PARKER*** GAINED THE PROPORTIONATE TRENGTH AND AGILITY OF A SPIDER! ARMED WITH HIS WONDROUS WEB-SHOOTERS AND COMMITTED TO USING IS AMAZING POWERS FOR GOOD, HE STRUGGLES WITH SINISTER SUPER-VILLAINS, MAKING ENDS MEET, AND AINTAINING SOME SEMBLANCE OF A NORMAL LIFE!

HERE NOW, BASED ON HIS ANIMATED TELEVISION SERIES, ARE...

THE ADVENTURES OF SPIDER-MAN

"...SO IF YOU'LL ***BE PATIENT*** FOR JUST A COUPLE MORE MOMENTS, LADIES AND GENTLEMEN, WE'LL ***START*** THE FIRST PART OF TODAY'S PROGRAM...

"...A PROGRAM YOU WILL ***UNDOUBTEDLY*** FIND BOTH ***ENTERTAINING*** AND ***EDUCATIONAL***!

"I SEE WE'RE GETTING THE ***'ALL SYSTEMS GO'*** SIGN FROM OUR TWO ***CONGENIAL HOSTS***, SO WITHOUT FURTHER DELAY...

"...LET'S GET ON WITH THE ***SHOW***!"

RHINO'S REVENGE

NEL YOMTOV WRITER
ANDY KUHN PENCILER
ROB STULL INKER
STEVE DUTRO LETTERER
KEVIN TINSLEY COLORIST
MARK POWERS EDITOR
BOB HARRAS CHIEF

THIS HISTORIC GATHERING IS BROUGHT TO YOU BY THE QUEENS SCIENCE INSTITUTE AND NASA--
--AND IT IS THE FIRST PUBLIC DEMONSTRATION OF IN-FLIGHT SPACE CONDITIONS SINCE OUR NATION'S "CONQUEST OF THE STARS" PROGRAM BEGAN OVER FORTY YEARS AGO.
VIDMAX, THE WORLD'S LARGEST VIDEO PROJECTION SCREEN, WILL ALLOW YOU TO SEE INSIDE THE CAPSULE AS THE BOYS PERFORM ROUTINE AND EMERGENCY PROCEDURES IN A STATE OF ZERO GRAVITY.
SUCH PROCEDURES CAUSE IMMENSE PSYCHOLOGICAL STRESS UNLESS DEALT WITH PROPERLY. OBVIOUSLY, THIS DUO HAVE DEVELOPED THEIR OWN, ER... "UNIQUE" WAY OF HANDLING THE PROBLEM...
SCIENCE INSTITUTE
"...MEET NEW YORK NATIVE COLONEL JOHN JAMESON OF VICTORY SHUTTLE FAME--
"--AND HIS CO-PILOT TERRY HEWLITT OF SUNNY MACON, GEORGIA!"
KEEPING AN EYE ON THINGS HERE SURE BEATS ANY OTHER DETAIL I'VE BEEN ON LATELY.
I DON'T KNOW, PHIL... SOMETIMES A CROWD THIS BIG CAN GET KINDA UNRULY...
YOU WORRY TOO MUCH, HANK. TRUST ME, WE AIN'T EVEN GONNA WORK UP A SWEAT...
HEY! I WANNA SEE SOME MTV UP THERE! THAT BALD GUY'S MAKIN' ME SICK!
IF YOU THINK HE LOOKS STUPID, GET A LOAD OF THAT JERK OVER THERE WHO'S PART OF THIS BOGUS SHOW!

I'M HERE FOR THE PRETTY MOVIE STAR ON THE SCREEN!
GET OUT OF MY WAY!
THAT'S NO ACTOR! THAT'S... THE RHINO!
RUN! RUN!
YAAGH!
I TOLD YOU FOOLS TO MOVE ASIDE!
BLAM
HE'S IN THE CLEAR NOW! FIRE! FIRE!
BLAM
SPING
GET THAT CAR!
--OUT OF MY WAY!
KRUNG
SPING
W-WHAT WAS IT I SAID ABOUT WORKING UP A S-SWEAT?
THERE'S THE CAPSULE! HE'S MINE FOR THE TAKING!

MY DAYS OF WAITING ARE OVER! THE TIME FOR REVENGE STARTS RIGHT HERE--
--RIGHT NOW!
YOUR BOSSES WERE PRETTY CARELESS ABOUT SECURITY, JAMESON! TAKING YOU IS ALMOST TOO EASY!
PWA SWOK
NO! NOT YOU AGAIN!
I'M FLATTERED YOU REMEMBER! LET'S GO!
NO! DON'T FIRE! YOU MIGHT HIT THE COLONEL I'LL CALL IN TO GET A TRACKING UNIT ON THEM!
YOU GET SOME BACK-UP DOWN HERE TO HELP WITH THE INJURED! HURRY!
THWAM
I'VE GOT A LOAD OF QUESTIONS I'VE BEEN DYING TO ASK, ASTROBOY, AND WITH THE ANSWERS I GET FROM YOU--
--I'M GOING TO DESTROY SPIDER-MAN!

...SO INSTEAD OF COMPLAINING, WHY DON'T YOU SHOW A LITTLE APPRECIATION?
TOMMYS R
IT'S NOT EVERY DAY I INVITE A FREELANCER TO BREAK BREAD WITH ME.
BESIDES, YOU SHOULD BE GRATEFUL I TOOK YOU TO A GENUINE NEWSMAN'S PLACE LIKE THIS!
UH, SORRY, MR. JAMESON, BUT I GUESS I'M JUST NOT VERY COMFORTABLE.
ALL THIS SMOKE! HOW CAN YOU BREATHE IN HERE?
YOU'RE SUCH A BABY, PARKER! THAT'S ONE OF THE REASONS YOU'LL NEVER BE A HARD-NOSED NEWSPAPER MAN LIKE ME AND THE REST OF THE GUYS AT TOMMY'S!
YOU'RE HOPELESS!
NOW LET'S GET ON WITH THE REVIEW OF THIS WEEK'S--
BEFORE THAT, JONAH, PETE WANTED TO ASK YOU SOMETHING. RIGHT, PETE?
R-RIGHT. Y'SEE, JJ... FINANCES ARE GETTING KINDA TIGHT. THERE'S SCHOOL TUITION, AUNT MAY'S MEDICAL BILLS, I NEED A NEW CAMERA... ANYWAY, I WAS HOPING FOR A RAISE--
A RAISE? FOR WHAT?
IT'S BEEN WEEKS SINCE YOU TURNED IN SOME EXCITING PHOTOS OF SPIDER-MAN! HOW DO YOU EXPECT ME TO AFFORD RAISES IF I CAN'T SELL NEWSPAPERS?
YOU'LL GET A RAISE WHEN YOU EARN IT... MAYBE!
BUT IT WOULD MEAN SO MUCH TO--
FORGET IT! END OF CONVERSATION! NOW ON TO IMPORTANT BUSINESS...
B-BUT--
I'VE GOT TWO EDITORIALS THAT ARE GOING TO PROVE THAT SPIDER-MAN'S NOTHING BUT A FRAUD!
WHAT ABOUT YOU, ROBBIE--
--WHAT'VE YOU GOT?
THERE'S THE PIECE ON THE PHYSICIST, DR. PEALE, WHO'S SYNTHESIZED A VIRUS THAT BREAKS DOWN AND "EATS" CHEMICAL COMPOUNDS.
WITH YOUR SCIENCE BACKGROUND, PETE, YOU MIGHT BE INTERESTED...
I'VE GOT MORE IMPORTANT THINGS ON MY MIND, ROBBIE...
...LIKE HOW I'M GONNA PAY ALL MY BILLS...

STOP SULKING, PARKER. A GUY LIKE YOU SHOULD BE GLAD TO EVEN HAVE A JOB! FACE IT, YOU JUST HAVEN'T BEEN PRODUCING LATELY.
MAYBE YOU'RE BURNED OUT FROM COVERING SPIDER-MAN. I'VE GOT AN IDEA...
HOW 'BOUT A NEW ASSIGNMENT... LIKE THE FLOWER SHOW AT THE JAVITS CENTER? HAH! EVEN YOU COULD HANDLE THAT...
EASE OFF, JONAH. LET'S DROP THE SUBJECT AND ENJOY LUNCH. SAY, ISN'T THIS STEW GREAT?
YEAH, REAL HAUTE CUISINE...
I BET OL' CHEAPSKATE JJ IS GONNA FIND SOME WAY TO STICK US WITH THE BILL...!
SORRY TO DISTURB YOU, SIR, BUT THERE'S A NEWS REPORT THAT CONCERNS YOU...
LOOK AT THIS! I'M A REGULAR NEWS MAGNET! PUT IT DOWN, MY GOOD MAN, SO I CAN SEE!
8
7
121679152
...THE SERENITY OF THE INSTITUTE'S SPACE EXHIBIT WAS SHATTERED BY THE SUDDEN AND VIOLENT APPEARANCE OF THE SUPER VILLAIN KNOWN AS THE RHINO...
...ALTHOUGH NO ONE WAS SERIOUSLY INJURED, THE RHINO DESTROYED THE 225 MILLION DOLLAR SPACE CAPSULE AND ABDUCTED AMERICA'S PREMIER ASTRONAUT...
...COLONEL JOHN JAMESON!
JOHN?! ABDUCTED? DEAR GOD! NO!
NO!
I'M GOING TO QUEENS TO HELP MY SON! YOU TWO PAY FOR LUNCH... I'LL GIVE YOU MY SHARE WHEN I GET BACK... REMEMBER...
...I ONLY HAD THE SALAD!

AT THAT MOMENT IN QUIET FOREST HILLS, QUEENS...

I CAN'T UNDERSTAND IT, MAY...

...YOU WERE FEELING SO WELL THE LAST FEW WEEKS. SUDDENLY, YOU'VE TAKEN ILL AGAIN.

HAVE YOU BEEN *FORGETTING* TO TAKE YOUR MEDICINE?

NO, *THAT'S* NOT IT, ANNA. I HAVEN'T BEEN *FORGETTING...*

THEN *WHAT*, AUNT MAY? WHAT'S WRONG? ARE YOU TELLING US *EVERYTHING?*

OH, NO! PLEASE DON'T TELL HIM! I DON'T WANT HIM TO WORRY ABOUT ME OR OUR FINANCES!

MAY, CALM DOWN. *PLEASE...*

HE'S SO *SENSITIVE!* HE MIGHT *GET SICK!*

PROMISE ME YOU WON'T SAY ANYTHING!

WE PROMISE, AUNT MAY, BUT ONLY IF YOU TAKE IT EASY. YOU'RE GOING TO GET SICKER IF YOU DON'T CALM DOWN AND TRY TO GET YOUR STRENGTH BACK.

C'MON, AUNT ANNA, MAY NEEDS REST...

WHY DID YOU PROMISE HER WE WOULDN'T TELL PETER?!

HE'S *ALREADY* UNDER TOO MUCH PRESSURE WORRYING ABOUT FINANCES, AUNT ANNA. THIS TIME *WE'LL* TAKE CARE OF MAY...

...RIGHT NOW, PETE'S GOT *OTHER* THINGS TO DEAL WITH...

HOLY--! WHAT A SCENE!
THE ENTIRE CITY IS GONNA LOOK LIKE THIS UNLESS I CAN STOP HIM SOON!
IT DIDN'T TAKE A BRAIN SURGEON TO FOLLOW THIS TIDAL WAVE OF DESTRUCTION TO THE RHINO, BUT NOW COMES THE HARD PART...
SHWOOSH
...HOW THE HECK DOES LITTLE OL' ME PUT THE SKIDS ON THE RUNAWAY FREIGHT TRAIN?
HEY, RHINO, DON'T YOU KNOW THE CITY'S GOT LAWS AGAINST LITTERING?
YOUR BOSS IS GONNA HAVE PLENTY OF FINES TO PAY!
SPIDER-MAN! SORRY TO DISAPPOINT YOU, BUT I'M SELF-EMPLOYED THESE DAYS...
Y'KNOW... I TRASH WHAT I WANT TO TRASH, KIDNAP WHO I WANT TO KIDNAP.
BUT MOSTLY, I DESTROY--

--WHO I WANT TO DESTROY!
KRA-DANG
HEADS UP, SPIDEY!
HE THREW THAT CAR LIKE IT WAS A CHILD'S RAG DOLL!
COULD HE HAVE GROWN EVEN MORE POWERFUL SINCE WE LAST FOUGHT?
BETTER PUT HIM TO THE TEST AND FIND OUT...
HEY RHINEY, REMEMBER HOW MY WEBBING SLOWED YOU UP LAST TIME?
THWIP
WELL, HERE'S A LITTLE BLAST FROM THE PAST TO JOG YOUR MEMORY, BIG GUY!
ARHH! YOU WHIPPED MY BUTT ONCE BEFORE, WEB-MAN... CAUSED ME TO LOSE MY JOB WITH THE KINGPIN...
...WORD GOT AROUND THAT I WAS LOSING MY EDGE... WASHED UP...
...GOING SOLO IS PHASE ONE TO SHOW PEOPLE THAT IT'S ALL LIES...
SNAPP
ARRGH! ALL LIES!
PHASE TWO WILL BE THE ANNIHILATION OF... YOU.
COMING THROUGH, SPIDER-MAN!
WAAAAAARRR
THIS IS LIKE TRYING TO STOP THE 5:15 EXPRESS WITH A BUTTERFLY NET!

OOMPH!
YOUR TIME HAS RUN OUT, BUG-EYES!
RAM
I THOUGHT EVEN YOU WOULD PUT UP A BETTER FIGHT...
...TO THINK OF ALL THE TROUBLE I WENT THROUGH...
...KID-NAPPING THE ASTRONAUT... HIDING HIM AWAY SOME-PLACE...
...I GUESS I DON'T NEED HIS HELP AFTER ALL!
AIEEE!
SK-ZAK
THAT SHOULD KEEP HIM DOWN... FOR A WEEK OR TWO!
WAIT! NO! IT CAN'T BE! H-HE'S GETTING UP!
NICE TRY, SPIDER-MAN. MAYBE NOW YOU'RE BEGINNING TO REALIZE WHAT I ALREADY KNOW AS FACT...

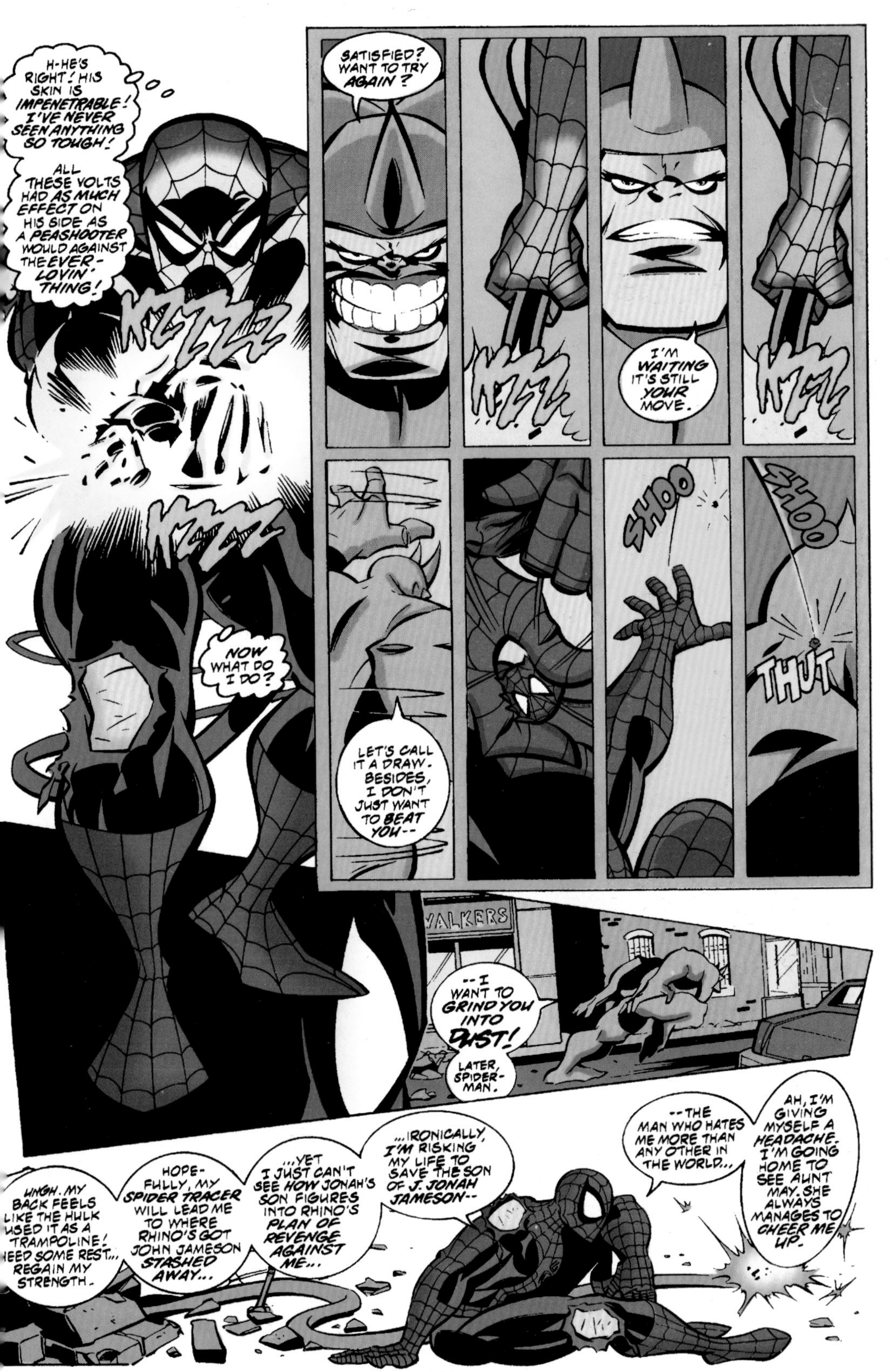
H-HE'S RIGHT! HIS SKIN IS IMPENETRABLE! I'VE NEVER SEEN ANYTHING SO TOUGH!
ALL THESE VOLTS HAD AS MUCH EFFECT ON HIS SIDE AS A PEASHOOTER WOULD AGAINST THE EVER-LOVIN' THING!
KZZZZ
KZZZ
SATISFIED? WANT TO TRY AGAIN?
KZZZ
I'M WAITING IT'S STILL YOUR MOVE.
KZZZ
NOW WHAT DO I DO?
LET'S CALL IT A DRAW. BESIDES, I DON'T JUST WANT TO BEAT YOU--
SHOO
SHOO
THUT
WALKERS
--I WANT TO GRIND YOU INTO DUST!
LATER, SPIDER-MAN.
UNGH. MY BACK FEELS LIKE THE HULK USED IT AS A TRAMPOLINE! NEED SOME REST... REGAIN MY STRENGTH.
HOPE-FULLY, MY SPIDER TRACER WILL LEAD ME TO WHERE RHINO'S GOT JOHN JAMESON STASHED AWAY...
...YET I JUST CAN'T SEE HOW JONAH'S SON FIGURES INTO RHINO'S PLAN OF REVENGE AGAINST ME...
...IRONICALLY, I'M RISKING MY LIFE TO SAVE THE SON OF J. JONAH JAMESON--
--THE MAN WHO HATES ME MORE THAN ANY OTHER IN THE WORLD...
AH, I'M GIVING MYSELF A HEADACHE. I'M GOING HOME TO SEE AUNT MAY. SHE ALWAYS MANAGES TO CHEER ME UP.

THE PARKER RESIDENCE...
SURE FEELS GOOD TO BE HOME. BEING AWAY FROM THAT HUMAN HOWITZER IS JUST WHAT I NEED...
HEY, AUNT MAY! YOU HOME? AUNT MAY!
DOCTOR LIEBER?! WHAT ARE YOU DOING HERE? IS ANYTHING WRONG WITH MY AUNT?
SHE'S HAD A RELAPSE, SON. ANNA WATSON TOLD ME THAT MAY STOPPED TAKING HER MEDICINE.
BUT W-WHY?
SHE SAID SHE COULDN'T AFFORD IT ANYMORE!
...NO BYSTANDERS WERE INJURED DURING THE TWENTY-MINUTE BRAWL BETWEEN SPIDER-MAN AND RHINO...
HER CONDITION IS SERIOUS--AND IT COULD HAVE BEEN AVOIDED! IF FINANCES ARE TIGHT--
--YOU SHOULD HAVE SAID SOMETHING! THIS IS INEXCUSABLE!
THINGS'VE BEEN LEAN, DOCTOR, BUT I NEVER DREAMED THAT SHE'D DO SOMETHING LIKE THIS!
I-I'M SO SORRY...
HOW COULD I LET THIS HAPPEN TO AUNT MAY? SHE'S ALL I HAVE IN THE WORLD... GOTTA HELP HER... GET MY HANDS ON SOME CASH!
BUT HOW?
YOU SHOULD KNOW THAT UNLESS TREATED QUICKLY, HER AILMENT WILL GET MUCH WORSE... IT COULD EAT AWAY AT HER!
YOU'RE NOT EVEN LISTENING TO WHAT I'M SAYING!
"EATS AWAY"? OF COURSE, WHY DIDN'T I THINK OF THAT?
L-LOOK, DOC, NOW THAT MAY IS OKAY, I GOTTA RUN A COUPLE OF ERRANDS.
I'LL CALL YOU LATER...
WHAT KIND OF NEPHEW ARE YOU? HOW CAN YOU RUN OUT ON YOUR AUNT LIKE THIS?
PROBABLY A BAD ONE FROM THE LOOKS OF IT, DOC, BUT I'VE GOTTA SET THIS RIGHT!

MANHATTAN...
UNNOTICED BY ANY LIVING SOUL, A BIZARRE SCENE UNFOLDS ON THE DARKENED MIDTOWN STREETS...
I'M TELLING YOU THE TRUTH, YOU STUPID OX! I REALLY DON'T KNOW ANYTHING YOU'RE TALKING ABOUT!
YOU'RE LYING! YOU SAW IT ALL! YOU WERE THERE!

MAYBE THE PROMETHEUM X ISOTOPE THAT KINGPIN HAD ME STEAL FROM THE SHUTTLE YOU CRASH-LANDED TURNED OUT TO BE NOTHING--
--BUT I SAW THE BLACK SLIME ATTACKING YOU ON TV WHEN YOU TRIED TO LAND. THAT'S WHAT I WANT YOU TO TELL ME ABOUT! NOW!
I DON'T KNOW WHAT THAT STUFF WAS! MAYBE IT CAME FROM THE PROMETHEUM! WHY DO YOU WANT THAT USELESS BLOB ANYWAY?
IT'S NOT USELESS! HAVEN'T YOU WONDERED WHERE THAT SUPER POWERFUL BLACK COSTUMED SPIDER-MAN--THE ONE CALLED VENOM--CAME FROM?
THE SLIME HAD TO BE RESPONSIBLE FOR IT! I WANT YOU TO TELL ME WHERE I CAN GET SOME...
...AND WHEN I DO, IT'S GOING TO MAKE ME FASTER AND STRONGER THAN I ALREADY AM! I'LL BE UNSTOPPABLE!

YOU'RE INSANE, RHINO! WHATEVER THAT STUFF WAS, SPIDER-MAN TRAPPED IT IN A SPACE LAUNCH AND SENT IT BACK TO THE COSMOS!
YOU CAN'T GET ANY MORE OF IT! IT'S GONE... FOREVER!
LIAR! YOU'RE STILL NOT TELLING THE TRUTH!
LET'S YOU AND ME FIND A COZY PLACE TO TALK MORE ABOUT THIS, COSMO BOY. YOU BETTER START TO REMEMBER...
...BECAUSE IF YOU DON'T, NASA WON'T BE SENDING YOU TO OUTER SPACE... THEY'LL BE SENDING YOU TO THE COUNTY MORGUE!
...

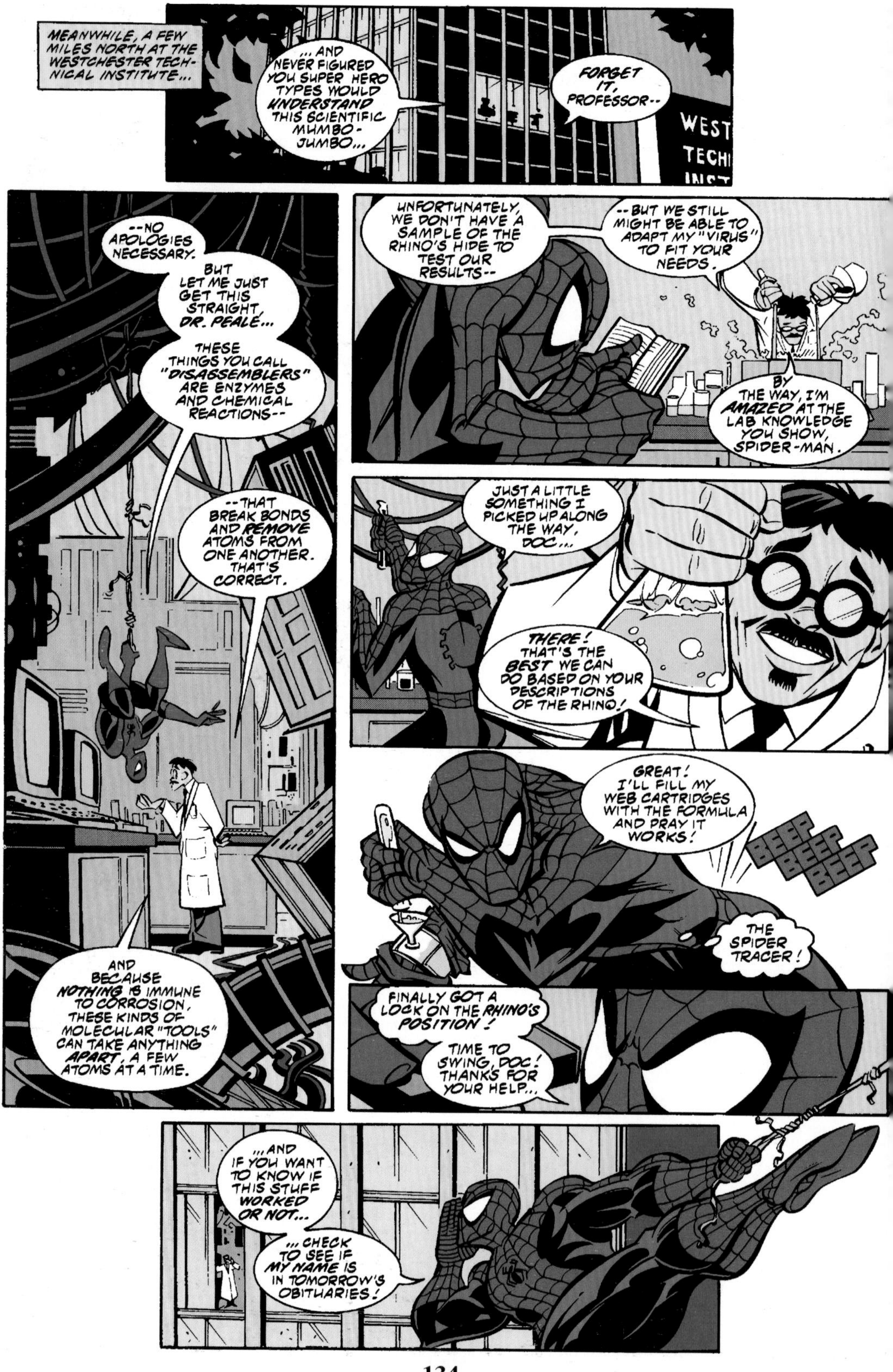

--NO APOLOGIES NECESSARY.

BUT LET ME JUST GET THIS STRAIGHT, DR. PEALE...

THESE THINGS YOU CALL "DISASSEMBLERS" ARE ENZYMES AND CHEMICAL REACTIONS--

--THAT BREAK BONDS AND REMOVE ATOMS FROM ONE ANOTHER. THAT'S CORRECT.

AND BECAUSE NOTHING IS IMMUNE TO CORROSION, THESE KINDS OF MOLECULAR "TOOLS" CAN TAKE ANYTHING APART, A FEW ATOMS AT A TIME.

UNFORTUNATELY, WE DON'T HAVE A SAMPLE OF THE RHINO'S HIDE TO TEST OUR RESULTS--

--BUT WE STILL MIGHT BE ABLE TO ADAPT MY "VIRUS" TO FIT YOUR NEEDS.

BY THE WAY, I'M AMAZED AT THE LAB KNOWLEDGE YOU SHOW, SPIDER-MAN.

JUST A LITTLE SOMETHING I PICKED UP ALONG THE WAY, DOC...

THERE! THAT'S THE BEST WE CAN DO BASED ON YOUR DESCRIPTIONS OF THE RHINO!

GREAT! I'LL FILL MY WEB CARTRIDGES WITH THE FORMULA AND PRAY IT WORKS!

BEEP BEEP BEEP

THE SPIDER TRACER!

FINALLY GOT A LOCK ON THE RHINO'S POSITION!

TIME TO SWING, DOC! THANKS FOR YOUR HELP...

...AND IF YOU WANT TO KNOW IF THIS STUFF WORKED OR NOT...

...CHECK TO SEE IF MY NAME IS IN TOMORROW'S OBITUARIES!

WITHIN MINUTES...
THERE HE IS! GOOD OL' SPIDER-TRACER COMES THROUGH AGAIN!
THE GOOD NEWS IS THAT THIS TIME RHINO'S GOT JOHN...
...THE BAD NEWS IS THAT I'M NOT GONNA BE ABLE TO RESCUE HIM WITHOUT TAKING ON HORN-HEAD!
I'LL POSITION MY CANON HERE AND SET IT ON AUTOMATIC.
AND NOW-- IT'S SHOWDOWN TIME!
THWIP
HEY, RHINO, DIDYA EVER THINK ABOUT GETTING AROUND TOWN IN A TAXI?
SPIDER-MAN! I WASN'T EXPECTING TO SEE YOU SO SOON, BUT AS LONG AS YOU'RE HERE--
THOK
LET'S DO IT!
WHOOPFF!

FLIP
FLIP
I LET YOU OFF EASY TODAY, SPIDER-MAN...
...BUT NOW IT'S NO MORE MR. NICE GUY!
SORRY WE'VE LOST SUCH A GREAT HUMANITARIAN, RHINO!
HEY!
KRAK
THESE GAMES AREN'T HELPING YOU TO MAKE ANY FRIENDS AT THE SANITATION DEPARTMENT, RHINEY!
SPEAKING OF GAMES...
HOW 'BOUT WE PLAY...
...TAG?
YOU'RE IT!
PKOW
I GOT A BETTER IDEA, WALL-CRAWLER...
ISN'T IT TIME YOU HAD--
--A V-8?!

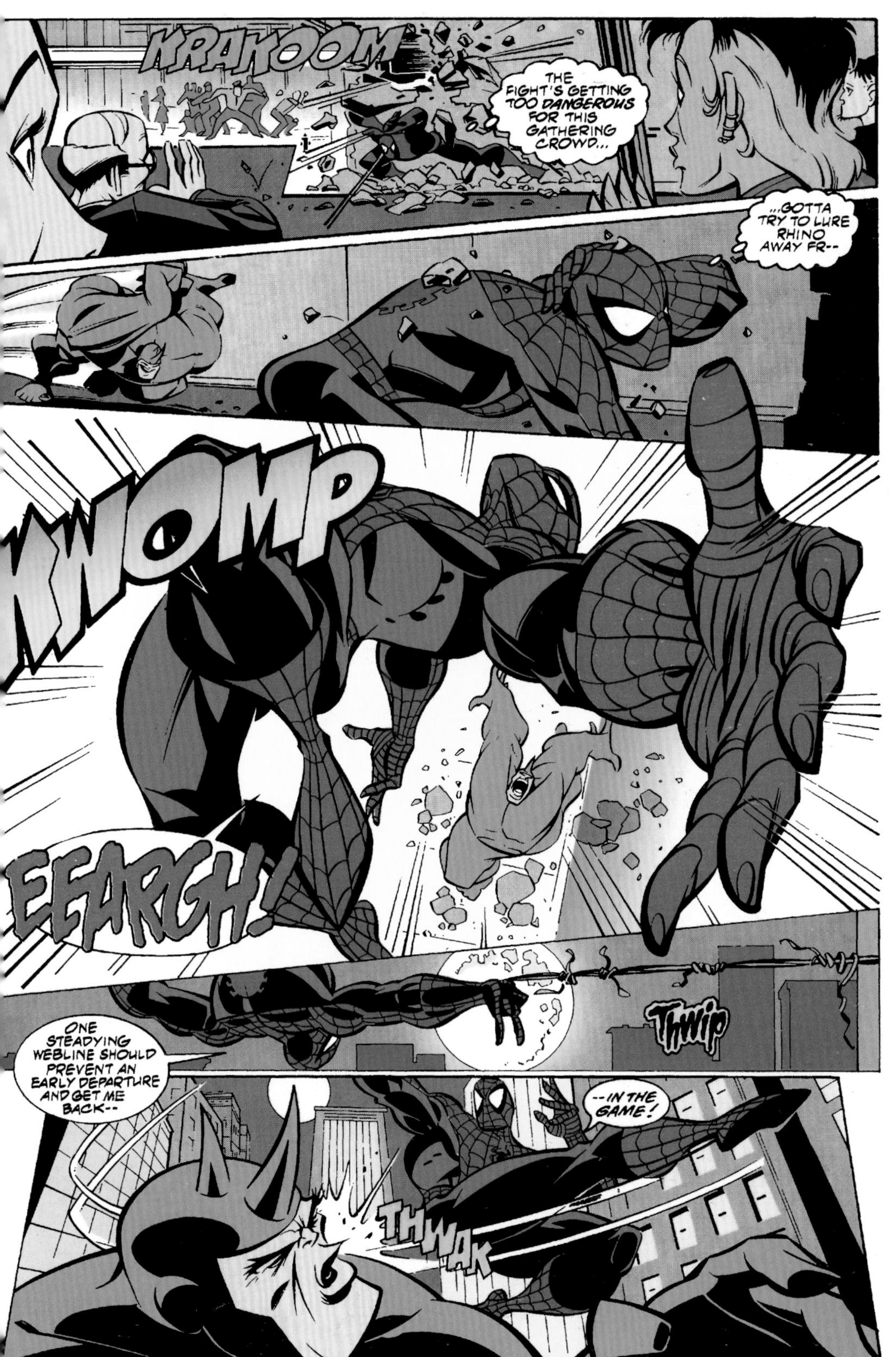
KRAKOOM
THE FIGHT'S GETTING TOO DANGEROUS FOR THIS GATHERING CROWD...
...GOTTA TRY TO LURE RHINO AWAY FR--
WOMP
EEARGH!
ThWip
ONE STEADYING WEBLINE SHOULD PREVENT AN EARLY DEPARTURE AND GET ME BACK--
--IN THE GAME!
THWAK

TAXI
GET OUTTA MY CAB! GET OUT, YOU MANIAC!
SORRY, PAL--HAD TO GET HERE IN A HURRY!
BESIDES, JUST LOOK AT THE TIP I'M LEAVING YOU... IT'S ALMOST FIVE PERCENT!
WHOAA! I CAN'T KEEP DODGING HIS ASSAULT FOREVER! CAN'T PUT OFF TAKING THE RISK...
...THE TIME TO TAKE A CHANCE ON DR. PEALE'S FORMULA HAS...
KRAK
SPLUGG!
--COME!
YOUR STUPIDITY ASTOUNDS ME! HAVEN'T YOU LEARNED THAT YOUR GREATEST WEAPON--YOUR WEBBING--
--IS USELESS AGAINST ME?
DON'T PLAY ME FOR A FOOL, SPIDER-MAN...
...IT MAKES ME REAL ANGRY!
SHRPP
I'M JONAH JAMESON, BLAST IT! LET ME THROUGH! MY SON'S IN TERRIBLE DANGER!

PEALE'S FORMULA IS WORKING! THE STUFF IS EATING THROUGH HIS HIDE!
DON'T LOOK NOW, RHINEY, BUT YOUR SKIN IS BEGINNING TO FALL APART LIKE A CHEAP SUIT!
GOT ANY MORE WORTHLESS TRICKS YOU WANT TO TRY, BUG-EYES?
NO, THAT WAS IT, RHINO. WHO DO YOU THINK I AM... THE AMAZING KRESKIN?
ARRGH!!
W-WHAT?! MY HIDE... IT'S DISSOLVING!
SKIN FEELS WARM...
GOTTA KEEP HIM OCCUPIED UNTIL THE FORMULA TAKES FULL EFFECT!
COME HERE, YOU PUNY RUNT!
N-NO! I'M STARTING TO BURN! FEELS LIKE I'M ON FIRE! CAN'T STAND THE PAIN!
BROTHER, YOU DON'T KNOW WHAT REAL PAIN FEELS LIKE...

THIS... IS REAL PAIN!
EEYARGH!

STAND BACK, FOLKS. THERE'S NOTHIN' MORE TO SEE. GO ON HOME.
OUT LIKE A LIGHT. HE WON'T BE DOING ANY STOMPING AROUND FOR A LONNNG TIME.
THE POLICE CAN TAKE THINGS FROM HERE...
...I'VE GOT A COUPLE OF OTHER THINGS TO CHECK ON.
NO, I'M OKAY, SPIDEY. BUT IF MY FATHER DESPISES YOU SO MUCH, HOW COME YOU'RE ALWAYS HELPING ME?
'CAUSE YOU'RE A GREAT GUY, COLONEL. YOU CAN'T HELP IT IF YOUR DAD'S A JERK!
AND SPEAKING OF THE OL' TIGHTWAD...
JOHN! STOP HIM! I WANT HIM QUESTIONED BY THE AUTHORITIES ABOUT THIS SCAM!
OH, BROTHER, HERE HE COMES. YOU THINK I COULD GO WITH YOU, SPIDEY?
MAYBE NEXT TIME, JOHN. I GOT A PACKAGE WAITING FOR ME TO PICK UP...
YIKES! MY CAMERA! IT'S GONE!
THE WEBBING'S ALMOST TOTALLY DISSOLVED! THE SPECIAL FORMULA STOPPED RHINO, BUT IT COULDN'T EVEN HOLD UP MY CAMERA!
WITHOUT ANY PHOTOS, I'LL NEVER GET THE CASH WE NEED! WHAT AM I GONNA DO NOW?
WHAT'S WRONG WITH ME? I JUST STOPPED 700 POUNDS OF UNBRIDLED FURY, SAVED A CITY FROM TOTAL DESTRUCTION, AND RESCUED AN AMERICAN SPACE HERO!
WHY DO I HAVE SO MUCH TROUBLE MANAGING MY OWN LIFE?

DAILY BUGLE
OKAY, MR. I-WANT-A-RAISE, BIG MOUTH... YOU HAD YOUR CHANCE. NOW TELL ME...
...WHERE IN BLAZES ARE MY GREAT PHOTOS OF SPIDER-MAN FIGHTING THE RHINO?
ER, WELL JONAH, YOU'LL NEVER BELIEVE THIS--
SPIDER-MAN ALMOST GETS MY SON KILLED IN A CHEAP PUBLICITY STUNT AND WE DON'T EVEN HAVE PICTURES TO NAIL HIM?!
HEY! LOOK AT THIS! THE NY PRESS SCOOPED US ON THE FIGHT IN THIS MORNING'S EDITION! GREAT FRONT PAGE PHOTOS, TOO!...
...COURTESY OF MR. PETER PARKER!
HUH?
THIS LETTER'S FOR YOU, PETE.
T-THANKS, ROBBIE.
WHAT IN BLAZES ARE YOU TRYING TO PULL, PARKER?
WOW! IT'S FROM JASON PHIPPS, PUBLISHER OF THE PRESS. LISTEN TO THIS...
...OUR REPORTER COVERING THE FIGHT FOUND YOUR CAMERA ON THE STREET... KNOWING YOU'RE A FREELANCER, I THOUGHT YOU WOULDN'T MIND SEEING YOUR WORK IN PRINT...
...ATTACHED PLEASE FIND A CHECK FOR YOUR PHOTOS WHICH I TRUST IS SATISFACTORY... ANYTIME YOU WANT TO JOIN THE PRESS, PLEASE CALL. WE CAN ALWAYS USE SOMEONE WITH YOUR TALENTS!
I'VE NEVER MADE THIS KIND OF CASH WORKING FOR YOU, JONAH! THIS SOLVES ALL OF MY MONEY PROBLEMS!
I'M GOING OVER THERE RIGHT NOW TO SPEAK WITH PHIPPS ABOUT A JOB!
W-WAIT, PARKER... DON'T BE SO HASTY! LET'S TALK ABOUT THIS! IF IT WAS MORE MONEY YOU WANTED, ALL YOU HAD TO DO WAS ASK!
PARKER!
DON'T WORRY, I'D NEVER LEAVE JONAH. IF I WAS GONE--
--WHO'D BE LEFT TO BRING SO MUCH JOY INTO HIS LIFE?
NEXT ISSUE:
THE HUMAN TORCH!

MARVEL® COMICS

NEW STORIES BASED ON THE HIT TV SHOW!

APPROVED BY THE COMICS CODE AUTHORITY

THE ADVENTURES OF SPIDER-MAN®

SPIDER-MAN

SEP. '96 6

ONLY 99¢

CLOBBERIN' TIME!

KUHN 5-96

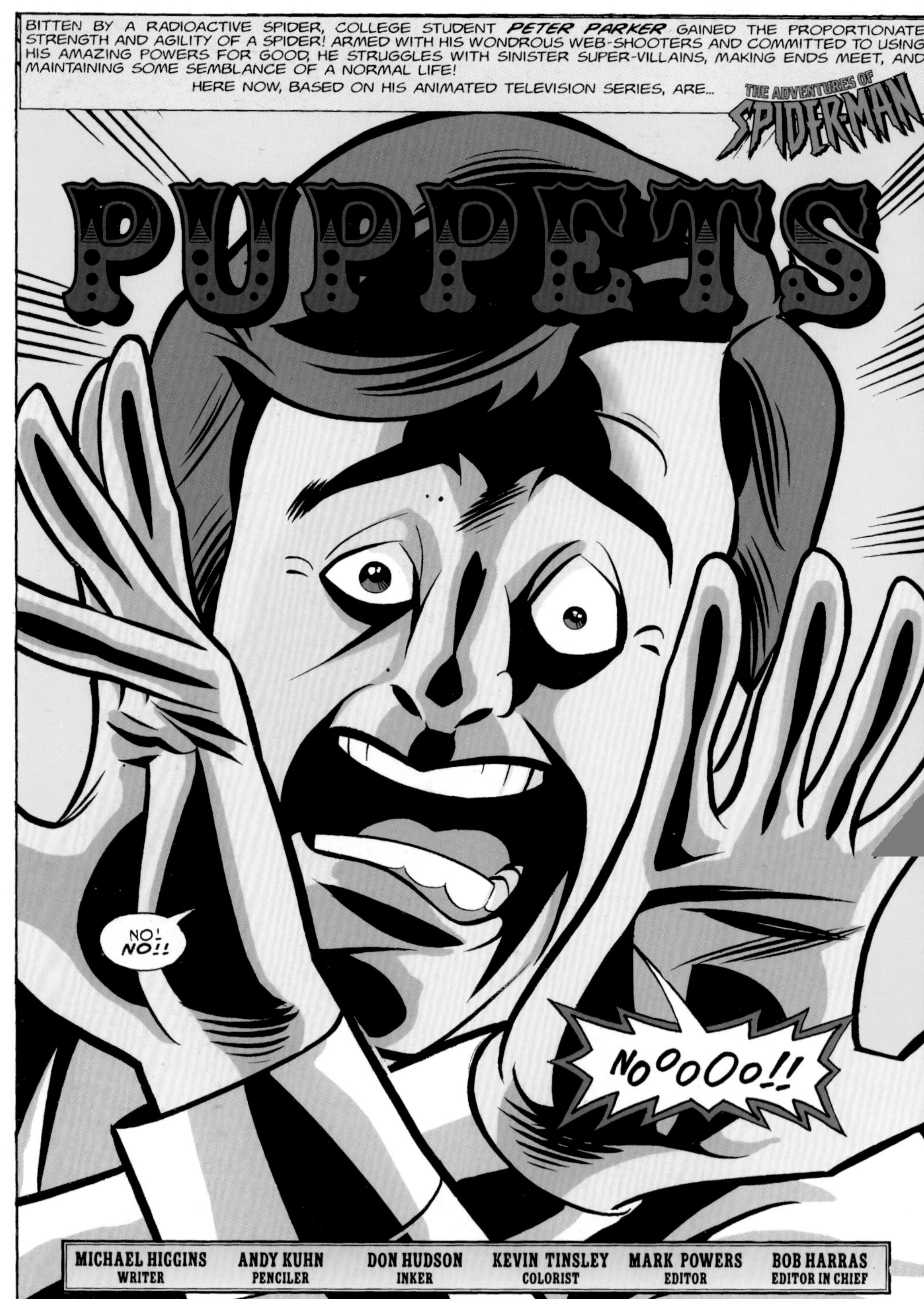
BITTEN BY A RADIOACTIVE SPIDER, COLLEGE STUDENT PETER PARKER GAINED THE PROPORTIONATE STRENGTH AND AGILITY OF A SPIDER! ARMED WITH HIS WONDROUS WEB-SHOOTERS AND COMMITTED TO USING HIS AMAZING POWERS FOR GOOD, HE STRUGGLES WITH SINISTER SUPER-VILLAINS, MAKING ENDS MEET, AND MAINTAINING SOME SEMBLANCE OF A NORMAL LIFE!
HERE NOW, BASED ON HIS ANIMATED TELEVISION SERIES, ARE...
THE ADVENTURES OF SPIDER-MAN
PUPPETS
NO! NO!!
NOOOOO!!
MICHAEL HIGGINS WRITER
ANDY KUHN PENCILER
DON HUDSON INKER
KEVIN TINSLEY COLORIST
MARK POWERS EDITOR
BOB HARRAS EDITOR IN CHIEF

NEVER, MR. JAMESON!
NEVER!!!
NEVER, PARKER? NEVER CAN BE A LONG TIME...
... A VERY LONG TIME...
... ESPECIALLY WHEN YOU'RE GOING WITHOUT A PAY-CHECK!
WITHOUT GULP A CH-CHECK?!
THAT'S RIGHT, PARKER...OR HAVE YOU FORGOTTEN YOU WORK FOR ME?!
AT LEAST--
--YOU USED TO!
B-BUT, MR. JAMESON-- YOU CAN'T DO THIS!
CAN'T, PARKER?
CAN'T?!
NOW GET THIS STRAIGHT, PARKER. I CAN DO ANY-THING I WANT AROUND HERE. I'M THE PUBLISHER!
AND IF YOU WANT TO KEEP YOUR JOB, YOU'RE THE NEW SOCIETY PAGE PHOTOGRAPHER WHILE MISS LIEBOWITZ IS OUT OF TOWN!
BUT I'M AN ACTION PHOTOGRAPHER! THE TYPE OF PICTURES I TAKE--
THE TYPE OF PICTURES YOU TAKE, I DON'T WANT ANY-MORE!
I'VE SEEN ENOUGH SHOTS OF THAT CONFOUNDED WEB-SLINGER, SPIDER-MAN, TO LAST THIS LIFE-TIME...
...AND THE ONE AFTER IT!
FWOOSH

KAFF! HAKK! KOFF!
LISTEN, PETER, MY BOY! IT MIGHT NOT BE AS BAD AS YOU THINK--
--HOBNOBBING WITH THE RICH AND FAMOUS!
SURE KAFF! I KOFF BET!
YOUR FIRST ASSIGNMENT WILL BE TOMORROW...
...AN ART EXHIBITION FEATURING THE WORK OF A BLIND SCULPTRESS NAMED ALICIA MASTERS.
IT'S OVER AT FOUR FREEDOMS PLAZA--THE SAME PLACE WHERE THOSE OTHER COSTUMED CLOWNS LIVE--
--THE FANTASTIC FOUR!
PUBLISH

AND ONE MORE THING, PARKER! YOU CAN'T SHOW UP AT ONE OF THESE SNOOTY EVENTS DRESSED LIKE THAT!
WHAT IS IT WITH YOU KIDS, ANYWAY?
DO SOMETHING ABOUT THOSE CLOTHES, WILLYA?
OH, I'LL DO SOMETHING ABOUT THESE DUDS, ALL RIGHT...

...BUT NOT THE WAY "JOLLY" JONAH THINKS!
6TH FLO
AND TOMORROW I'LL WORRY ABOUT--

"--FOUR FREEDOMS PLAZA!"
NO PARKING
HEY, BEN! THERE'S AN ARTICLE IN THE DAILY BUGLE ABOUT ALICIA'S EXHIBIT!
NO KIDDIN'? HOW DO YOU LIKE THAT, ALICIA?
IT'S LIKE I ALWAYS SAY--
--BABY, YOU'RE THE GREATEST!
I ALWAYS KNEW IT! NOW THE REST OF THE WORLD DOES, TOO!
SAY, WHERE DO YOU WANT ME TO PUT THIS... THING?
AS CUTE AS HE MAY BE--AND AS MUCH AS I'M GONNA HATE TO SAY GOOD-BYE TO HIM--
WHAT? HE AIN'T HEAVY...HE'S YOUR BROTHER?
THAT WOULD EXPLAIN WHY HE'S JUST AS UGLY AS YOU!
LIBERTY
LISTEN, MATCHSTICK, I'LL GIVE YA UGLY IF YOU WANNIT!
BOYS! THAT WILL BE ENOUGH OF THAT!
THE MAD THINKER!
ALICIA MASTERS
I'LL HAVE NO MORE OF YOUR BICKERING WITH THE HUMAN TORCH...
...GIVEN EVERYTHING THAT HAS TO BE DONE BEFORE THE OPENING TOMORROW!

THERE'S STILL SO MUCH TO DO!
JUST SAY THE WORD, BABY, AND I'LL CALL REED AND SUE* AND TELL THEM I GOTTA STAY HERE WITH YOU!
*MISTER FANTASTIC AND THE INVISIBLE WOMAN -- THE HUMAN TORCH AND THING'S TEAMMATES IN THE FANTASTIC FOUR.
I WOULDN'T HEAR OF IT, BENJAMIN J. GRIMM!

REED AND SUE ARE INVOLVED IN SPECIAL GOVERNMENT WORK-- AND THEY NEED YOU!
THERE'S NOTHING TO DISCUSS, YOU MUST GO!
OKAY, BABY, BUT YOU KNOW WHAT THAT MEANS!
THE HOTSHOT OVER HERE IS GONNA HAVE TO FILL IN FOR ME AS YOUR ESCORT TOMORROW!
I REALIZE HE'S NOT MUCH OF A REPLACEMENT FOR A REAL MAN, BUT--

A REAL MAN, Eh?
WELL, I'LL SHOW YOU!

HOW ABOUT A LITTLE FIRE, SCARECROW?
CRIPES! WHADDAYA THINK YER DOIN'?
FWOOSH
THIS AIN'T NO WIZARD OF OZ--

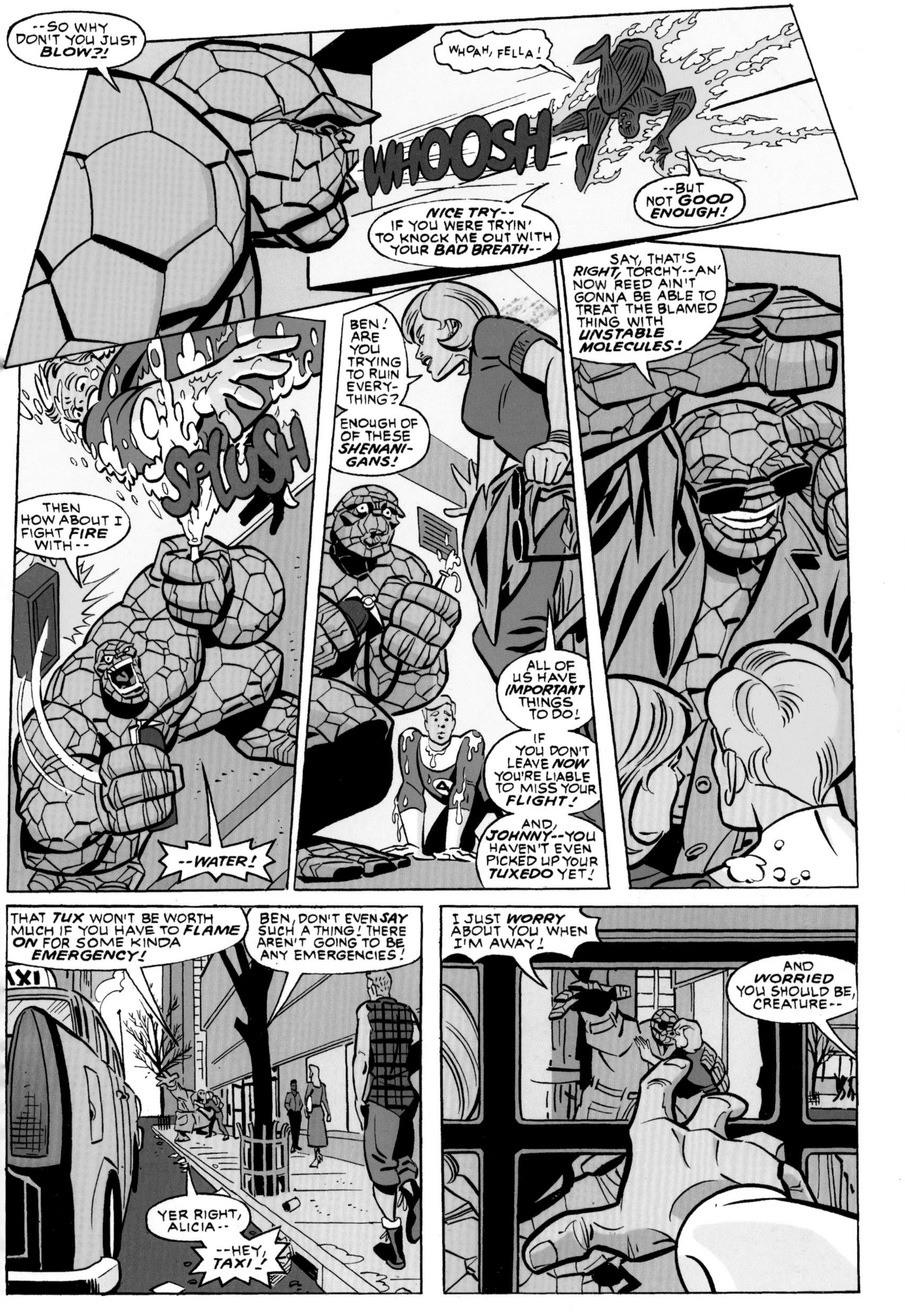

--SO WHY DON'T YOU JUST **BLOW?!**

WHOAH, FELLA!

WHOOSH

NICE TRY-- IF YOU WERE TRYIN' TO KNOCK ME OUT WITH YOUR **BAD BREATH--**

--BUT NOT **GOOD ENOUGH!**

SPLUSH

THEN HOW ABOUT I FIGHT **FIRE** WITH--

--WATER!

BEN! ARE YOU TRYING TO RUIN EVERY-THING?

ENOUGH OF OF THESE **SHENANI-GANS!**

ALL OF US HAVE **IMPORTANT** THINGS TO DO!

IF YOU DON'T LEAVE **NOW** YOU'RE LIABLE TO MISS YOUR **FLIGHT!**

AND, **JOHNNY**--YOU HAVEN'T EVEN PICKED UP YOUR **TUXEDO** YET!

SAY, THAT'S **RIGHT,** TORCHY--AN' NOW REED AIN'T GONNA BE ABLE TO TREAT THE BLAMED THING WITH **UNSTABLE MOLECULES!**

--IN MATTERS THAT CONCERN MY DAUGHTER!
A PITY-- FOR THEM-- THAT THEY GO ABOUT THEIR BUSINESS, THE UNSUSPECTING PAWNS IN A GAME BEYOND THEIR COMPREHENSION--
--A GAME THAT WILL BE WON BY THE PUPPET MASTER!
A GAME THAT BEGAN WHEN I WAS A YOUNGER MAN...
...ALMOST IDEALISTIC--
TOGETHER WITH MY CLOSEST FRIEND, A COLLEAGUE FROM MY UNIVERSITY DAYS, I DISCOVERED FISSIONABLE MATERIALS THAT WERE THE SO-CALLED BUILDING BLOCKS OF LIFE.
IT WAS A QUEST THAT WENT ASTRAY--
--FOR THERE WAS MORE INVOLVED THAN MERE FRIENDSHIP FOR JACOB REISS-- THERE WAS THE MATTER OF HIS WIFE, MARCIA, AND HIS CHILD, ALICIA--
--AND THE JEALOUSY WHICH FILLED ME WHEN I THOUGHT OF HIM RECEIVING HER LOVE-- A LOVE WHICH I WANTED-- BUT COULD NEVER HOPE TO HAVE!
"THE PAIN GREW AND GREW...
"...BUT THEY NEVER KNEW THE BURNING RESOLVE THAT HAD CAUGHT FIRE IN MY BREAST--
"--A RESOLVE TO DESTROY WHAT JACOB AND I HAD BUILT TOGETHER--FOR IN MY FRUSTRATION, I COULD THINK OF NO OTHER WAY OUT!
"AND ONE NIGHT, WHEN I'D PLANNED TO BE ALONE AT OUR LAB-- IT HAPPENED!

"HE'D SEEN THE LIGHT FROM THE ROAD AND HE WAS CONCERNED THAT SOMETHING WAS WRONG-- BUT WHEN HE SAW WHAT I WAS DOING, HE AT LAST UNDERSTOOD!
"WHILE WE STRUGGLED, THE VATS BEHIND US CONTAINING OUR PRECIOUS RADIOACTIVE CLAY CONTINUED TO BUBBLE AND BOIL, BUILDING TO CRITICAL MASS.
"FINALLY, I PUSHED HIM BACK! HE HIT THE RAIL AND IT WAS DONE!
"HOW COULD I HAVE KNOWN THAT HIS WIFE AND CHILD WOULD CHOOSE THAT MOMENT TO LEAVE THEIR CAR TO STEP DIRECTLY INTO THE BLAST!
"MARCIA WAS UNCONSCIOUS, BUT UNINJURED...BUT WHEN ALICIA FINALLY OPENED HER EYES, THEY STARED UNSEEING!
"MARCIA NEVER KNEW HOW JACOB DIED. BELIEVING HER CHILD NEEDED A FATHER, SHE ACCEPTED MY LOVE AND WE SOON MARRIED!"
BUT THINGS CHANGED WHEN ALICIA'S MOTHER DIED, AND I DISCOVERED THAT BY USING PUPPETS FROM CERTAIN CLAY MIXTURES I COULD CONTROL THE MINDS OF THEIR REAL-LIFE COUNTERPARTS!
THAT WAS WHEN THE GAME TRULY BEGAN-- A GAME THAT WILL END IN NOTHING LESS THAN MY DOMINATION OF THE ENTIRE WORLD!
BUT TOO OFTEN HAVE I-- AND MY ERSTWHILE PARTNER, THE MAD THINKER-- RUN AFOUL OF THE ACCURSED FANTASTIC FOUR!
BUT WE HAVE LEARNED FROM PAST ERRORS!
ALL THAT IS GOING TO CHANGE, MY DEAR!

"THE FANTASTIC FOUR ARE TOO STRONG WHEN FACED AS A TEAM! THEY MUST BE DIVIDED IN ORDER TO BE CONQUERED AT LONG LAST!"
AN ART EXHIBIT!
HOW COULD SOMETHING LIKE THIS HAPPEN TO ME?!
I'M JUST--
--A REGULAR GUY!
PETER, IS THAT YOU?
I DIDN'T EVEN HEAR YOU COME IN!
PETER, YOU LOOK SO PALE!
AREN'T YOU FEELING WELL?
IS SOMETHING WRONG?
OH, NOT REALLY, AUNT MAY! IT'S JUST THIS DUMB ASSIGNMENT I GOT FROM THE DAILY BUGLE!
STARTING TOMORROW, INSTEAD OF TAKING PICTURES OF SPIDER-MAN, JAMESON WANTS ME TO WORK ON THE SOCIETY PAGE AND I JUST--
OH, PETER! THAT'S WONDERFUL! NO MORE PICTURES OF THAT AWFUL SPIDER-MAN!
YOU'RE STARTING TO GET SOMEWHERE IN THE WORLD!
YOU DON'T UNDERSTAND, AUNT MAY!

I UNDERSTAND PERFECTLY, DEAR, AND DON'T WORRY!
I'M HERE TO HELP YOU!
YOU'LL BE NEEDING A NICE, NEW SUIT!
DEAR ME, HOW WILL WE EVER GET IT BY TOMORROW?
PERHAPS THAT NICE MR. KRUCHKOW AT THE TAILOR SHOP WILL DO ME A SPECIAL FAVOR!
OH, THIS IS SO EXCITING!
HOO-BOY!
AND, SO...
JUST A MINUTE, PETER -- WHERE ARE YOU GOING?
I'M ON MY WAY TO SEE THE TAILOR!
NOT SO FAST!
NOT WITHOUT ME-E-E-E-E-E-E!
STOP, AUNT MAY! YOU DON'T HAVE TO COME!
I'M PERFECTLY ABLE TO SHOP FOR MY OWN CLOTHES --
-- ALONE.
AS MUCH AS I LOVE MY AUNT, THIS IS CERTAINLY ONE TIME I DON'T NEED HER AROUND!
THIS IS EMBARRASSING!
WELL, ONE THING'S FOR SURE! MY LIFE COULDN'T GET ANY--

--WORSE!
OH, NO! WHAT'S HE DOING HERE?
THAT'S JOHNNY STORM, THE HUMAN TORCH!
HE USED TO DATE DORRIE EVANS FROM SCHOOL. I'D RECOGNIZE HIM ANYWHERE!
I JUST HOPE HE DOESN'T RECOGNIZE--
--ME!
WELL, WELL! IF IT ISN'T PUNY PARKER!
HAVEN'T CHANGED A BIT, HAVE YOU, STORM?
WHY MESS WITH SUCCESS? THIS IS THE WAY THE GALS LOVE ME!
DON'T WORRY, MRS. PARKER. THEY'LL BE ABLE TO FIND SOMETHING FIT YOUR NEPHEW.
THEY HAVE SOME WONDERFUL CLOTHING HERE IN THEIR BOYS DEPARTMENT!
HERE YOU ARE, MISTER STORM. COME ANY TIME...
...AND ENJOY THE OPENING!
OPENING?!
YEAH. TOMORROW NIGHT BEN'S GIRLFRIEND IS HAVING A SHOW AT FOUR FREEDOMS PLAZA.
FOUR FREEDOMS PLAZA?
IT CAN'T BE!
TA-TA, PARKER! SEE YOU AROUND!
'FRAID SO, TORCH--AND SOONER THAN YOU THINK!

AND, THE FOLLOWING DAY...

I DON'T BELIEVE IT! PETER PARKER-- AGAIN?!

WHEN I SAID I'D SEE YOU AROUND... I DIDN'T REALLY MEAN IT!

WHAT HAPPENED, PARKER? DID YOU GET LOST?

YOU DON'T BELONG IN A CLASSY CROWD LIKE THIS!

WHAT ARE YOU DOING HERE?

WHAT DOES IT LOOK LIKE, EINSTEIN?

SQUIRTING A TOY CAMERA?

LET ME MAKE IT EASY FOR YOU! JUST SMILE, SAY "CHEESE" AND TRY TO LOOK INTELLIGENT FOR THE CAMERA!

I GATHER THE TWO OF YOU HAVE MET BEFORE...?

OH, YEAH. WE'RE... Ahem... OLD FRIENDS.

THEN WHY DON'T YOU COME WITH US, MR. PARKER, AND TAKE A FEW SHOTS WHILE WE MINGLE WITH THE CROWD?

HEY, BOOKWORM, IF YOU PLAY YOUR CARDS RIGHT, MAYBE SOME-DAY YOU, TOO, WILL BE DATING A GLAMOROUS CELEBRITY!

WHO ARE YOU KIDDING, STORM?
EVERYBODY KNOWS MISS MASTERS IS THE THING'S GIRL, SO QUIT YOUR BRAGGING!
JUST BECAUSE HE COULDN'T MAKE IT, DOESN'T MEAN--

REALLY, GENTLEMEN! DO I HAVE TO SEPARATE THE TWO OF YOU?
THIS IS MY BIG NIGHT--

-- AND I DON'T WANT ANYTHING TO GO WRONG!
I'M SORRY, FELLA, BUT YOUR NAME ISN'T ON THE LIST!
YOU WEREN'T INVITED!
YOU CAN'T COME IN!
I ALREADY TOLD YOU...
HUNH?! MY SPIDER-SENSE IS TINGLING!
...I NEED NO INVITATION!
THAT VOICE!
OH, NO! IT CAN'T BE! NOT HIM!
NOT HERE-- NOT NOW!
WHATEVER'S HAPPENING...
... IT LOOKS LIKE IT'S TIME FOR PETER PARKER TO BAIL OUT!
I'M GETTING OUT OF HERE!
ME, TOO!
GO AHEAD, PARKER-- RUN!
RUN, YOU COWARD!!!
JUST LIKE PUNY PARKER TO SPLIT AT THE FIRST SIGN OF TROUBLE, EH, ALICIA?
ALICIA, WHAT'S GOING ON?
ALICIA!
ALICIA?!?

DON'T WORRY, YOUNG FOOL!
SHE IS "SAFE" IN THE ARMS OF HER LOVING FATHER!
YEAH, WELL, WE'LL SEE HOW LONG THAT LASTS!
MUST... DO AS HE... SAYS...
FLAME ON!
YIKES! BEN WAS RIGHT!
I SHOULD HAVE THOUGHT ABOUT THOSE UNSTABLE MOLECULES!
OH, WELL! NOTHING I CAN DO ABOUT IT NOW!
HUNH? SOMETHING DARTING PAST ME!
SOMEONE ELSE ATTACKING?
NOT AT ALL, FRIEND!
I JUST FIGURED YOU COULD USE A HELPING HAND!
SPIDER-MAN!*
* THE HUMAN TORCH DOESN'T KNOW PETER PARKER IS SPIDER-MAN.
I RELEASE YOU, PUPPET!
NOW FLEE LIKE THE REST OF THE RABBLE --

--BEFORE I CHANGE MY MIND!
HE'S STILL GOT ALICIA, SO WE HAVE TO BE CAREFUL--
--BUT WE CAN'T LET HIM TURN THAT TO HIS ADVANTAGE!
ALL RIGHT, BALDY! LET'S SETTLE THIS THE EASY WAY!
RELEASE THE GIRL AND SURRENDER!

YOU KNOW THAT WOULD BE FAR TOO SIMPLE, TORCH--
--AND THE BATTLE HAS JUST BEGUN!
FATHER-- NO!

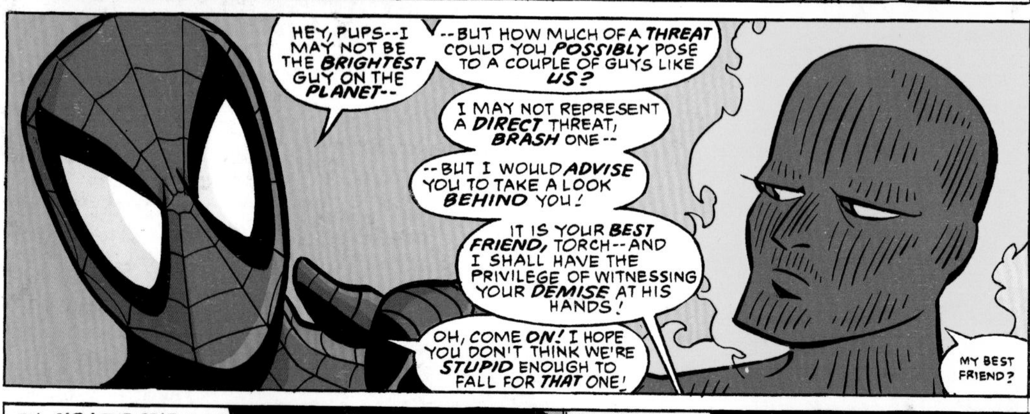
HEY, PUPS--I MAY NOT BE THE BRIGHTEST GUY ON THE PLANET--
--BUT HOW MUCH OF A THREAT COULD YOU POSSIBLY POSE TO A COUPLE OF GUYS LIKE US?
I MAY NOT REPRESENT A DIRECT THREAT, BRASH ONE--
--BUT I WOULD ADVISE YOU TO TAKE A LOOK BEHIND YOU!
IT IS YOUR BEST FRIEND, TORCH--AND I SHALL HAVE THE PRIVILEGE OF WITNESSING YOUR DEMISE AT HIS HANDS!
OH, COME ON! I HOPE YOU DON'T THINK WE'RE STUPID ENOUGH TO FALL FOR THAT ONE!
MY BEST FRIEND?

OH, NO! THE STATUE OF "LIBERTY"! THE NAME WAS CARVED ACROSS THE BASE WHEN WE WERE SETTING UP YESTERDAY--
--AND NOW IT'S GONE!
AND SO IS THE STATUE!
WHICH MEANS IT WASN'T A STATUE OF THE THING AT ALL--

--IT WAS THE REAL THING!
A SOFT DRINK?
HEY!
SHOULDN'T SOMEONE HAVE SAID--
--"IT'S CLOBBERIN' TIME"?!
KBLAM
BEN IS FIGHTING LIKE... WELL... LIKE A MAN POSSESSED--
--AND WITH GOOD REASON, SEEING HOW THAT'S PRETTY MUCH WHAT HE IS!
WE'VE GOT TO FIND SOME WAY TO CONTAIN HIM--
--WITHOUT ACTUALLY HURTING HIM!
AND I GUESS THE WALL OF FLAME--

--YIKES--
--ISN'T GOING TO DO THE JOB!
FATHER, YOU MUST PUT AN END TO THIS MADNESS!
MADNESS?! I THINK NOT, CHILD!
I AM ON THE VERGE OF ULTIMATE TRIUMPH!!
THEN IF YOU WON'T STOP IT--
--I WILL!
LET'S SEE IF A LITTLE BIT OF WEBBING WILL SLOW THE BIG GUY DOWN!
THWIP
FATHER, I CANNOT BELIEVE YOU WOULD DO SUCH A THING TO THE MAN I LOVE.
WHAT DO YOU KNOW OF LOVE?
LOVE CAN ONLY LEAD TO MISERY!
IF ONLY YOU COULD SEE HOW TRULY WRONG YOU ARE!
LOVE IS THE STRONGEST THING THERE IS...
...AND THROUGH OUR LOVE, WE WILL FIND A WAY TO DEFEAT YOU!
DO YOU HEAR ME?
THIS IS THE MAN I LOVE AND--
NO!!!
THIS IS NOT BEN AT ALL! IT IS NOTHING BUT A SOULLESS, LIFELESS CONSTRUCT-

THAT INFORMATION, I'M AFRAID, WILL BE OF LITTLE VALUE TO YOU--
--FOR THERE IS A NEW PAWN IN MY GAME!
WHOAH! WHAT'S HAPPENING TO ME...?
AND WE STILL HAVE NOT SEEN THE LAST OF YOUR "LOVE"!
SHRAP
C'MON, SPIDEY!
NOT YOU, TOO!
SPIDEY?
SPIDEY?
GREA-A-A-AT.
NOW I'VE GOT TWO OF THEM ON MY TRAIL!

HEY, WAITAMINNIT!
TWO OF THEM?
THAT'S IT!
AND NOW IT'S TIME TO TURN THEIR STRENGTH--
--TO MY ADVANTAGE!
JUST GOT TO POSITION MYSELF THE RIGHT WAY AND--
ALLEZ-- OOOOP!
KLA
BLAMMM

FWUMMMP
UNNGGH!

NO! THE SPIDER-MAN PUPPET! IT MUST BE--
THUD THUD

IT MUST BE ELIMINATED!

AND I'LL GO SUPER-NOVA AND OBLITERATE THIS DOPPELGANGER!
SHLUCCH

NO!
HOW DID YOU KNOW?!
HOW COULD YOU POSSIBLY BE CERTAIN--

--THAT THE MAD THINKER ACTUALLY CONTROLLED THE ANDROID--
--THROUGH A SURGICALLY-IMPLANTED, BIO-CHEMICALLY POWERED, HIGH FREQUENCY, PULSE-CODE MODULATED RADIO-LINK?!
WELL... I DIDN'T KNOW THAT!
AND AT FIRST, I WASN'T SURE ABOUT WHAT ALICIA SAID ABOUT THE CONSTRUCT...
...ESPECIALLY GIVEN WHAT PUPPET MASTER SAID ABOUT MY BEST FRIEND... AND THE WAY IT LOOKED EXACTLY LIKE THE REAL THING.
BUT PUPPET MASTER CAN'T CONTROL TWO MINDS AT ONCE...
...SO WHEN IT BECAME OBVIOUS THAT HE WAS CONTROLLING SPIDER-MAN...
...I KNEW HE COULDN'T ACTUALLY BE IN CONTROL OF BEN AT ALL!
KNOWING IT WASN'T BEN, I WAS FREE TO CUT LOOSE WITH THE FULL FORCE OF MY POWER!
THE MAD THINKER--WHO WAS "HIDING" HERE IN PLAIN SIGHT ALL ALONG--MUST HAVE CONSTRUCTED IT WITH THE AID OF THE PUPPET MASTER AND HIS RADIOACTIVE CLAY.
YES... THE RADIOACTIVE CLAY!
I MUST HAVE SOME--
--IMMEDIATELY!
IF I CONCENTRATE... ITS UNIQUE PROPERTIES...
...COUPLED WITH THE ENERGIES OF THIS DEVICE...
...WILL ENABLE A MOST OPPORTUNE RETREAT!
FAREWELL, FOOLS!
WE SHALL MEET AGAIN!
SOME SORT OF IMPENETRABLE GLOBE HAS FORMED AROUND THEM!
AND I'VE GOT NEWS FOR YOU--
--IT'S BLASTING OFF!
IT ISN'T GOING ANYWHERE WITHOUT US!
NO PARKING

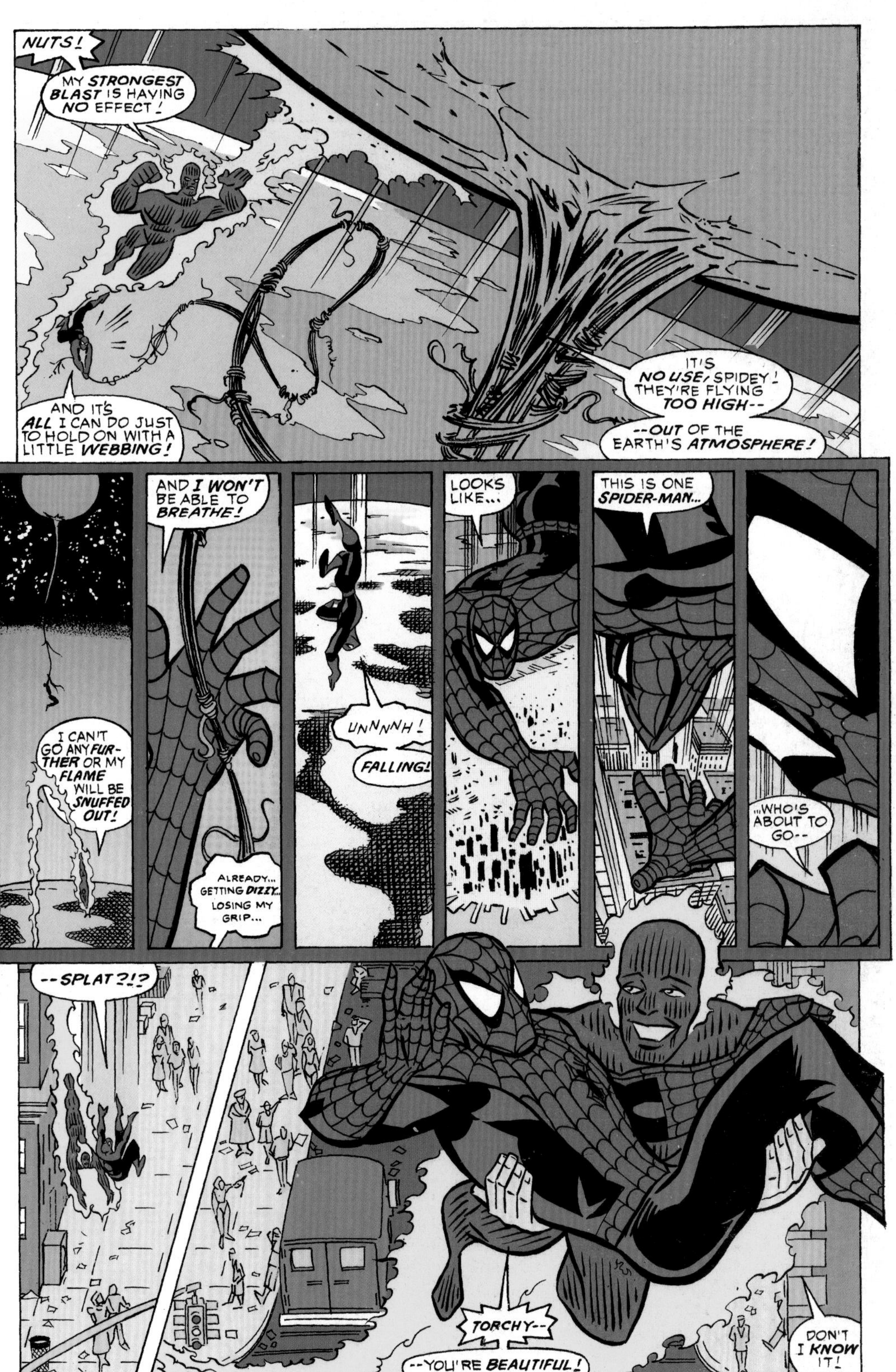
NUTS!
MY STRONGEST BLAST IS HAVING NO EFFECT!
AND IT'S ALL I CAN DO JUST TO HOLD ON WITH A LITTLE WEBBING!
IT'S NO USE, SPIDEY! THEY'RE FLYING TOO HIGH--
--OUT OF THE EARTH'S ATMOSPHERE!
I CAN'T GO ANY FURTHER OR MY FLAME WILL BE SNUFFED OUT!
AND I WON'T BE ABLE TO BREATHE!
ALREADY... GETTING DIZZY... LOSING MY GRIP...
UNNNNH!
FALLING!
LOOKS LIKE...
THIS IS ONE SPIDER-MAN...
...WHO'S ABOUT TO GO--
--SPLAT?!?
TORCHY--
--YOU'RE BEAUTIFUL!
DON'T I KNOW IT!

Y'KNOW, SOMETIMES HE CAN ACT LIKE SUCH A JERK...
...BUT WHEN THE CHIPS ARE DOWN...
...THIS IS THE MAN I WANT IN MY CORNER!
FLAME--
--OFF!
FLAME OFF?
HEE-HEE!
FLAME OFF?!?
HA! HA! HA! HA! HA!
OKAY, YOU LAUGHING HYENA! SUPPOSE YOU TELL ME WHAT THE BIG JOKE IS!
OH... LET'S JUST SAY IT'S A GOOD THING FOR YOU THAT I LEFT A BUNDLE OF CLOTHES UP HERE WHEN I CHANGED INTO COSTUME EARLIER!
WHAT ARE YOU TALKING ABOUT?
COME ON, JOHNNY.. THINK!!
AREN'T YOU FORGETTING SOMETHING?
OH, NO! MY TUXEDO!
IT BURNED OFF-- AND I NEVER HAD A CHANCE TO GET INTO MY UNIFORM!
I'M NOT...
GULP
...WEARING ANYTHING!
HERE YOU GO, BIG FELLA!
IT LOOKS LIKE YOU NEED THESE A LOT MORE THAN I DO!
THE END